Beast

Ally Kennen
AR B.L.: 3.9 Alt.: 632
Points: 8.0

UG

BEAST

GO THERE.

OTHER TITLES AVAILABLE FROM PUSH

BEAST

ALLY KENNEN

SCHOLASTIC INC.

NEW YORK TORONTO LONDON AUCKLAND SYDNEY

MEXICO CITY NEW DELHI HONG KONG BUENOS AIRES

ISBN-13: 978-0-439-86550-0
ISBN-10: 0-439-86550-6

12 11 10 9 8 7 6 5 4 3 2 1   7 8 9 10 11 12/0

Printed in the U.S.A.   40
First PUSH paperback printing, October 2007

For Dan Amos
with love x

ONE

Here is a list of the ten worst things I have done:

1.   Bullying: age seven. Forced my three-year-old brother, Chas, to smoke a cigarette.

2.   Theft: age eight. Stole one hundred and twenty pounds of pension money from my gran's handbag.

3.   Theft and slaughter: age eight. Nicked my first car (a Ford Fiesta) with my older brother, Selby, and crashed it into an old man's garden, killing the birds in his aviary. (Eight was a bad year for me.)

4.   Trespassing: age ten. Crapped on my head teacher's doorstep after he kicked me out of primary school.

5.   Emotional cruelty: age eleven. Told my father (my real one) that I wished he would die so I'd never have to see him again.

6.   Arson: age twelve. Lit a fire in a trash can in the playground, which spread to three classrooms.

7.   Perversion: age thirteen. Nicked a neighbor's white, lacy bra from her clothesline.

8. Deception: age fourteen. Went door-to-door collecting money from old people saying it was for starving children.

9. Biohazard sabotage: age fifteen. Spat results of bad cold into my foster sister's mango face cream to inflict small revenge.

10. Murder: age seventeen. I haven't done it yet.

Number ten on my list is going to be the worst yet and it's taking a lot of planning. I still don't know if I'll go through with it. I know it's wrong to end a life. No matter how evil that life is. But I'm running out of choices and going slowly crazy.

I buy one pig a month. I can't afford any more than that. I've no idea whether this is enough, but it keeps him alive. He's still growing and this is a worry.

I go to four or five different butchers. Some are more expensive than others. Jimmy, my foster dad, always wants to know what I'm spending my money on. I'm pretty sure he suspects I have a drug problem. Nice, isn't it? He keeps dropping hints and leaving leaflets around. If he knew I was spending the money on pork he'd be really shocked.

Today I pull up outside Thorney's butchers in Bexton. Before I get out of the car I look around a bit to see if I recognize anyone. But football is on the telly and the street is pretty much deserted.

Thorney is a small blond man who wears jeans under his white, blood-spattered coat. He eyes me up as I walk through the hanging chains into his shop. It smells of blood and cleaning fluid. I see Thorney has a special offer on homemade beef sausages.

"Is it a big party?" he asks.

I feel confused. What party? Then I remember. In the past I've said that I work for a company that supplies pigs for hog roasts.

"Not especially big," I say. "Why?"

He doesn't answer and beckons me to follow him. I go behind the counter and into the back of the shop. There's a kettle and a microwave and an old office chair that looks like it has come out of the trash. There is also a safe in the wall and the door is open a little bit. I can't see inside. We go down a few steps to a set of steel doors. Thorney pulls them open and I get a rush of cold air in my face. There are shelves of meat, and freezers that have clear doors, with packets of mince and sausages inside, as well as a lot of stuff I can't recognize. The carcasses of pigs, sheep, and half a cow hang from metal S-shaped hooks. The floor is sticky beneath my shoes. It's also freezing and my breath comes out in clouds.

"This is yours," says Thorney, pointing to a massive headless creature. Its guts have been torn out and its trotters removed. "He's not properly thawed yet, so make sure he gets at least another day before he's cooked."

The animal dangling in front of me is far bigger than I ordered, and I tell Thorney so. But he only shakes his head. "This is all I've got, son. Take it or leave it."

I have no choice but to take it. I haven't fed him for over four weeks and I'm worried he'll start making a racket. Sometimes he roars when he smells me coming. What if he is doing it now, pressed up against the bars of his cage? What if someone goes to see where the noise is coming from?

We carry the pig up the stairs together and the flesh is cold and slippery beneath my fingers. I hope I have enough money to pay for it.

Thorney wraps the pig in white plastic and helps me heave it into my car.

How the hell am I going to get the thing to the reservoir? I'll never manage it on my own. From the pull-over, there's a walk through a field and a climb over a six-foot fence before reaching the water. This is going to be a problem.

I slam the trunk down hard to make it shut.

I wipe sweat from my forehead and pay Thorney one hundred and thirty pounds and get into my car. I sit back and feel a trickle of relief. It always makes me nervous, buying these pigs. What if someone I know sees me?

Thorney knocks on the window and I wind it down.

"Most people like the head kept on for a hog roast," he says. "Are you sure your boss won't be returning this to me?"

"It's fine," I say, and switch on the engine.

The car cost me most of my savings. It is an old Renault 5. Five door. Silvery-blue. It's an old banger but I had to have it. I passed my test six months ago. I worked at the melamine factory every minute I could to buy it. And it's fully insured and everything. I'm legal. Everyone is surprised at me. I've never saved up for anything before. I even surprised myself. I've hardly got any money left now. Not with the price of pigs. I have to think of some other way of feeding him, because last week I lost my job at Quality Melamine Homewares.

I decide that I'll take the pig back to the house and cut it up. Then I'll be able to manage it. This might sound simple to you, but it isn't really. You see, my house isn't my home at all, even though I've lived there for three years. And the family isn't my real family. I am what is now known as a "Looked-after Child." When I was younger they called it "Being In Care."

I drive the three or four miles out of Bexton to the Reynoldses' house. Or should I say, My Current Home. They live pretty much in the sticks. At least by my standards they do. There's a pub and a couple of shops a bit farther on in Gruton, and that's it. I'll tell you about my foster father, Jimmy Reynolds, his wife, Verity, and their son, Robert (eleven) — later. At this precise moment I'm worried about running into the Reynoldses' daughter, Carol, age fifteen. Daughter of Satan. She doesn't miss much.

I pull off the road and park a little way up the gravel drive. It's about five o'clock in the evening. They've made the garden pretty nice: lots of flowers and a swing in the tree and no crappy gnomes or statues like my gran goes in for. The Reynoldses don't have any neighbors. This must be good, seeing as they've looked after kids like me and worse for so many years. Who would want to live next door to a house full of crazy teenagers? It's quite a large place. Everyone has their own room so there is enough space to get away from each other. I go indoors and wash my face in the kitchen sink. Then I make myself my favorite sandwich, which is cheese and brown sauce melted together on white bread in the microwave.

"Somebody's got BO," announces a shrill voice behind me.

Carol. I ignore her.

"It's disgusting," she continues. "Didn't your mother teach you to wash?"

I dry my hands on the tea towel to annoy her. Then Jimmy, her dad, comes in, and she seems to shrink into a pretty dark-eyed girl in red trousers and a pink T-shirt.

"Dad," she squeals. "That top does nothing for you."

5

"Cheeky," he says. He ruffles her hair and nods at me. He goes through to the conservatory where Verity is reading the paper. Carol turns and gives me a smug grin and flounces after him.

I sigh. I'm too old for this. I'm too old to be forced into other people's families like a jigsaw piece from a different puzzle. I've never fit in anywhere.

I am about to go upstairs when Carol sidles back into the room.

"You've got blood on your neck," she says. "Bleeding zit?"

I wave her away but she ignores me. I spit on my hand and wipe at my neck. Carol and Robert are always screaming at each other, and Verity and Jimmy let them get away with it. At home, me and my brothers always got a whack.

"We'll have to disinfect your room when you've gone," she says. She breaks into giggles and dances over the kitchen floor, her dark hair bouncing off her shoulders.

I have this belief: The more pink a girl wears, the more twisted and evil she is. Pink is Carol's favorite color. She ought to have grown out of it by now. The band in her hair and the stripe at the top of her socks are pink. Even her cat, Dudley, has to wear a pink, fluffy collar. It doesn't suit him. He's this ten-year-old gangster with no ears.

In my room I look at the telly and one by one I hear the family go upstairs.

At about ten o'clock there's a knock on my door. It's Jimmy.

"Everything all right?" he asks. He looks at the walls and very hard at the lumps in the unmade bed. He scans the carpet, searching for evidence of some unknown crime.

"Fine," I say, switching the channel with the remote.

"Any luck with the job hunting?"

"Nope."

Jimmy leans against the door. "You'll need one if you want to keep that car legal."

"Yep."

Jimmy says he'll leave me in peace and shuts the door quietly behind him.

He's all right, really. He's about fifty. His official title is "Foster Carer." He's had kids like me coming and going in his house for twenty-five years. He's seen it all. Or maybe not. I think of the dead animal in the trunk of my car, oozing blood into the carpet mats.

At two o'clock in the morning I pick up my flashlight and creep down the stairs. I tense at every creak because Carol has ears on stalks. She once caught me making a sneaky sandwich in the middle of the night and gave me such a look that anyone would have thought I was burgling the place.

Jimmy keeps his tools in the garden shed, which is always unlocked. I am amazed at this. You'd think that after having looked after kids like me for years he'd keep his saws and hammers and glue guns locked well away. I put the flashlight on the ground, open the trunk of my car, and somehow manage to get the pig on my shoulder. It's so heavy I can hardly breathe. The thing has thawed a bit. I begin to wonder if I'll make it to the shed. Everything hurts: my back, my shoulders, my neck. And my stomach feels like it is going to explode with the effort. My eyes begin to get used to the dark and I can see quite a lot. There is a half-moon lighting things up for me. When I reach the grass I

7

have to drop the carcass because my limbs have gone all tired and shivery and won't work properly. I look back at the moonlit house to see if anyone is watching, but the curtains are still. It is so quiet I can hear my heart beating. When I get my breath back I grab the wrapping and start dragging the thing. My fingers keep sliding off the plastic, and when I finally move it, the plastic rips, leaving the flesh exposed. I haven't got the strength to pick it up again, so I roll it over and over. It thumps on the grass and I worry the sound will wake the family. But I have to keep going. At the door of the shed I kneel and shove the thing with all my strength, gritting my teeth and shutting my eyes. The pig comes to a halt nestled between the lawn mower and a bag of cat litter. I've done it. I allow myself to rest for a few moments. I'm breathless and a little bit giddy but I feel full of energy. It's quiet outside. Nobody knows what I am doing. I am safe. But I'm never going to get a pig as big as this again. I tear open the plastic but leave it underneath to catch any spillage. It will be hard to explain away any stains. I go get my flashlight and find Jimmy's saw poking out of a bucket of tools. I fish it out and finger the serrated edge. I don't know where to begin cutting. I had this vague idea that I might somehow string the pig up and slice all the way down its backbone and cut the bloody thing in half. But the roof doesn't look strong enough to hold the weight, so I decide to start working on a leg instead. If I manage to get all four off, the main body of the pig will be lighter and easier to work with. Luckily for me the animal has already been gutted. I can't cope with messy intestines and stuff.

I kneel and put the blade on the cold flesh. I shudder. *Come on*, I tell myself, *you have to do it*. I shut my eyes and begin to saw. I am trembling and feel sick. I'll never be able to eat bacon again. As I saw, a metallic smell fills the shed and I have to turn away for a minute.

I once asked a butcher to cut up a pig for me. He said it would cost me ninety pounds. Now I know why. The flesh breaks quite easily since the legs have just about thawed, but then I get to bone and it feels like I am hacking away for hours, getting nowhere, covering myself with blood and fat and God knows what and feeling sicker and sicker every minute. I have an idea. I'll cut the pig where the bones join each other. Then I'll only have to saw through gristle and ligaments rather than bone. But it will mean starting all over again. I roll the pig over and feel around its shoulder. I resume work. I am getting hot, and when I wipe the sweat from my face, my hands are sticky.

Then I see a flicker of light out of the corner of my eye.

Someone is coming over the lawn, a flashlight beam bouncing off their feet. They'll be here in a few seconds. Can I hide what I am doing? I taste blood as I bite my lip. I have to do something. I pull myself to my feet and drop the saw. I open the door of the shed and close it carefully behind me. A white glare shines directly in my face.

"What are you doing in there?"

A silhouetted figure stands behind the flashlight.

"Stephen." Carol's voice wobbles. "You're all covered in blood."

TWO

Let me tell you something about Carol. Just so you know what I'm up against. She's what my gran would call a shit-stirrer. When I arrived three years ago, Carol got me into trouble in the first ten minutes. Jimmy was carrying my stuff up to my room and Verity was standing around chatting to me about schools and bedrooms and food. Robert came and had a stare but soon vanished when he saw there was nothing particularly astonishing about me. Verity went to answer the phone and only Carol remained, sitting at the head of the kitchen table and following my every move. She made a loud clicking noise with her teeth. She seemed to be thinking very hard. Then she fished something out of her pocket.

"Look at this," she said. "Do you think it's a forgery?" She passed over a twenty-pound note with a large pink ink stain just above the Queen's head.

I took it and held it up to the light. "Nah, look. It's got a watermark and the metal strip." I tried to give it back to her but she stood up.

"I think I've got one of those pens in my room," she said. "So you can tell if it's a forgery. Hang on a minute, will you?" And she was gone.

So I sat examining the note and feeling pleased that the family was turning out to be so friendly.

Verity bustled in, talking about food or something, and stopped dead. I don't know why I did it, but I scrunched the note up in my fist. For some reason I didn't want her to see me holding it.

But I was too slow.

"That's funny," said Verity slowly. "I've got a note with a mark on it like that in my purse." I followed her gaze to a handbag lying on the kitchen counter.

"It's not mine," I said quickly, and let the note fall to the table. "Your daughter gave it to me." I couldn't remember her name at the time.

"Really," said Verity. It wasn't a question. She checked in her purse, and sure enough the note was missing.

"She thought it was a forgery," I said. "She's just gone to get a special pen."

Verity looked at me very carefully. She looked disappointed. Eventually she spoke.

"Carol's just gone out. She won't be back till later," she said. She took the note from the table and folded it in her purse.

I had heard the front door close of course, but I never thought it was Carol.

"Bitch," I said out loud. She had fixed me up. Framed me, all within ten minutes of my being here.

"Sorry?" said Verity.

"Nothing," I said, and closed my eyes. I gave up. What was

the point? Verity had already cast me as a thief. And who could blame her?

I've been a thief all my life.

That was the first ten minutes I spent with the Reynolds family. Now I stand in the darkness, looking at Carol's small outline, and know I am sunk.

"I knew it would be you." She sounds scared but curious. She looks beyond me at the shed. "What's going on?"

My mind races to find an explanation.

"I found a massive spider crawling over my pillow," I say. Carol hates spiders. "So I brought it out here. I caught my arm on a nail."

"You're lying," she says. I can tell she's dying to go and look in the shed but is freaked out by the blood.

"Big spider," I say. "With hairy legs."

Carol lets out a half laugh. "You've been cutting yourself," she says. "I thought only girls did that." She pushes past me.

"Don't," I say desperately. "There's a surprise in there."

"I like surprises." Carol marches ahead.

I have no choice but to rush forward and block the doorway. "Do me a favor, Carol, and go back to bed."

"Yeah, right." She tries to shove me away, digging her fists into my stomach. But I am much bigger so she doesn't get anywhere.

"If you don't let me in, I'll go and get Mum and Dad."

She's getting angry. Her voice has gone squeaky and she's

giving me nasty little jabs with her knuckles. She pulls away from me and runs round to the side of the shed. Before I can stop her she's shining her flashlight through the window. I freeze, expecting a barrage of questions. Instead there is silence.

Then I hear a whimper. The flashlight snaps off and she is running back to the house.

"Mum, Mummy." Her voice gets louder as she reaches the door. "Oh, HELP." Her voice breaks into a scream. "*Murder.*"

I roll my eyes and enjoy a few moments of cool darkness. There is no way I can hide the pig now. I feel the breeze playing on my cheek and listen to the muffled noises coming from the house. One by one, the lights switch on. I wonder if this will mark the end of my stay with the Reynolds family. In a few hours I might be on the street. But won't they get punished by Social Services if they kick me out? It's only a dead pig, after all. It isn't as if I've committed a crime or hurt anyone. I haven't even stolen the pig. A weak feeling climbs up my legs, like I've had too much to drink, and I have to sit down. The wet grass soaks through my pants. I put my head in my hands and wait for the storm to break. It's no fun being me sometimes.

I hear voices.

"I'm going to call the police."

That's Verity. She sounds terrified.

"Carol was half asleep. There's bound to be a simple explanation."

Good old Jimmy. He really hopes I'm not as bad as he thinks. The porch lights go on and the garden is flooded in light and shadow. Jimmy looks out into the garden.

"Stephen," he calls. "Are you out there?" He sounds nervous.

"Yep," I say. I make myself stand. Jimmy is going to think every-thing is weird enough without me having some kind of breakdown.

He pads out over the grass. "I'm just coming over to have a chat with you, Stephen. Nothing to worry about. Carol's got her knickers in a twist about something."

"Fine," I say. And I step into the light.

Jimmy gasps. "What's that on your face?"

"Skin?" I volunteer, aware that I am smeared with pig.

Jimmy steps right up to me. "So what's all this about?"

I shrug. I mean, what would you say if you were me? I haven't thought of an explanation as to why I'm trying to cut up a whole dead pig in the middle of the night with a hacksaw. What can I say? "Oh, I wanted to see how they were made"? Or "I just found it here," or "It's my mate's"? None of these will do. For the moment I decide to remain silent. I will think of something. I usually do. By now Jimmy has pushed the door of the shed open and is shining his flashlight inside.

I hear a gasp.

I nod to myself. I would be fairly surprised too.

"Stephen?"

He's sounding a little too dramatic. I stand next to him and he moves away like he's scared of me. In the dim light I can see the alarm in his face as he shines the light on the finger-marked hacksaw and the pale pink pig flesh lying in the tarp on the floor.

He shines the beam right in my face and at my hands.

I am silent.

He leans back against the wall, breathing like he's just run up and down the stairs.

"It's not that bad," I venture.

Jimmy walks heavily to the door and takes a deep breath. "I'm going back to the house now. I want you to stay here. Don't follow me." He makes as if to go, then he turns.

"Who was she?"

I shrug.

"Just a pig."

I sense his shock.

He backs warily out of the shed. The tarp is covering most of the pig. All that can be seen is the long, naked back. I have an urge to laugh, and I believe I let out a chuckle. As you know, I am indeed planning a murder, but not yet, not yet.

"No, Jimmy, wait. It really *is* a pig."

But he is haring across the lawn. "Verity, keep the kids indoors and call the police."

I go after him. I don't want the police mixed up in this. I like to keep a low profile these days. Once the rozzers have an eye on you, you can't do anything. No, it is far better to remain unobtrusive, unknown. Out here the local police don't know who I am. I don't want that to change.

"Jimmy, I haven't killed anyone. It's a pig I got from the butcher."

Jimmy stops dead and slowly turns.

"What?" He looks at me for a long time. The door swings open and Verity stands there.

"A dead pig, that's all?" she asks.

"Yep," I say, cool as anything. "A one-hundred-pound porker. I got it in Bexton this afternoon."

Verity pushes past me and hurries to the shed.

"For God's sake, Jimmy," I hear her mutter.

15

I don't think Jimmy wants to leave me alone with his wife but he is desperate to check out the shed again.

"Chill out," I say. "What do you think I am anyway?"

I hear the faint rustle of plastic.

"Pig!" shouts Verity from the shed, and Jimmy runs to join her.

The beams of their flashlights flicker through the shed window. Back in the house, two faces press up against the glass of the front door. When they see me, they disappear. I feel bad then. I don't want to scare anybody. Well, not Robert anyway. I don't like to imagine what he must be thinking.

I sit on the garden swing and rock myself back and forth on my toes.

They're in there for ages.

Eventually they come out. I imagine that even in the darkness, I can see a look of shame on Jimmy's face.

"I'm not a murderer, Jimmy," I say quietly.

"What was I supposed to think?" he says, raising his hands helplessly. "I'm sorry."

But Verity is still in for the attack.

"Well?" she says. "What were you intending to do with it?"

I stand with as much dignity as I can.

"It's for my dad," I say. "He's starving."

THREE

I deliver the pig the following night. Jimmy even helps me load it into the trunk of my car. He also gives me a bag of flour, three apples, and two pints of milk. I will throw these away when I get the chance.

"Sure you don't want me to come with you?" he asks. He looks worried. There's nothing about this in his foster parents' handbook. I can see him mentally running through his options. Ought he to forbid me to go, or call my social worker?

I pull out of the drive and onto the road. As I change gears I laugh.

As if I would feed my starving father a dead pig!

It takes me about fifteen minutes to reach Gruton Reservoir. It's quite a big place. There's a path that takes you all the way round. I walked all six miles of it once. Not much there really, just a small fishing hut with an empty Coke machine and a loo, plus some rowboats pulled on the bank for the fishermen. There's always a few funny-looking geese bobbing around on the water, and wherever you look there are munching sheep. Gruton

Reservoir is surrounded by fields and trees, so it's pretty quiet. Years ago I went swimming here with some mates. It was freezing so I wasn't in very long. And I definitely don't fancy swimming in it now. The dam, though, is cool. You can walk right over it. One side is water and the other is a massive drop down to a valley. You'd definitely die if you jumped off.

I pass the public parking lot and pull off the shoulder a few miles farther on. It's quite dark by now and there's nobody about. The pig is in halves. Jimmy helped me to cut it. He said my dad wouldn't want the trotters and threw them away. Each half is in a trash bag inside a blue plastic sack, the sort Jimmy gets his wood delivered in. I heave a sack onto each shoulder and stagger to the gate. The pig is cold and slippery and some kind of fluid seeps out of the plastic and runs down my back. Halfway down the field I collapse. My shoulders ache and I've cut my finger. The stars are out. I sit in the wet grass sucking the blood from my finger. I'm alone with the wind and the dead pig. I let my mind go blank. I feel still and peaceful. If it was dry I could almost go to sleep. I shut my eyes and listen to the night. I hear the wind in the trees and a car on the road. I can hear some sort of bird screeching. Then I go cold.

I can hear him roaring in the distance.

There are no houses round here. But I'm still worried that someone might hear him. I hope he's roaring because he's smelled me, and not because he does it every night.

I drag the sacks down the slippery field. They slide over the ground and flatten trails in the grass. At the fence I heave one sack into my arms and try to throw it over. But it falls short of the fence and I have to shift so it doesn't land on me. The fence is eight feet high, and its metal links are too small for me to gain a decent foothold. But I scramble up, with a sack balanced on my shoulder. The pig smells really strong. It's not just blood, but also a musty smell, like rotting car seats. The sack catches on the wire at the top and rips. The meat tumbles out and falls to the ground. At least it's on the other side of the fence. I drop to the ground and skin the flesh from my palms. More blood. I suck at my hand.

Sometimes I wonder what would happen if I didn't feed him. Of course, it's likely he would starve to death. But I read once that he could possibly go without food for six months as long as he had enough water. The body would go into a kind of hibernation, then a deep coma. I read on the Internet that there were records of an individual surviving for a year without food, but that this was very rare. I imagine my boy sinking deeper into the mud, growing thin and weak. And one day, years later, someone might find his bones. But would he make a noise as he was starving? Would he get some kind of massive death energy and break out of his cage?

I picture a field of dead sheep and a dark shadow moving towards an isolated cottage. I imagine a baby crying.

He knows not to roar when it's light. At least, I hope he does. One morning I crept up on him. He must have heard me coming and slipped from his ledge into the water, because when I looked down through the bars, all I could see were ripples on the surface and a damp smear on the concrete where he'd been basking in the sun. So maybe he's scared of people. I wish.

I imprisoned him at the side of the reservoir four years ago.

I like walking over paths, not along them. I like to crawl

19

through fences and climb trees and take shortcuts through people's gardens. When I was a kid, me and Selby, my brother, used to go to High Street at night. There's a fire escape next to the old Telecom building, and if you climb the fence, you can get up there. At the top it's a short jump to the roof of the shopping mall, and from there we got to most of the roofs all along High Street. We'd sit up there, smoking and watching people. It was tempting to gob on people but we knew if we got caught we wouldn't be able to go up there again. It was our secret. Mine and Selby's.

So I'd wandered off the path, tracking a fox. (I was a bit of a sad case back then.) I followed it through some trees and long grass. It went right through this thorny hedge, and so did I. We came out into a clearing between a bank of brambles and some trees, and there was this funny building, half buried in the bank. There was a sign saying DANGER — KEEP OUT. Water gushed out of a hole in the front and ran down a channel into the reservoir. I forgot about the fox and went to investigate.

It was a kind of cage concreted into the bank, about fifteen feet long and rising about eight feet above the ground. It was all overgrown with brambles. The roof and sides were made of rusting metal bars and there was a hatch in the roof that was padlocked shut. A low concrete wall, covered in green moss, ran round the base. I looked down through the bars and saw that below ground level the cage was full of water. It looked deep. I couldn't see the bottom. Ledges of concrete stepped down into the water and a rusted pump mechanism hung, half submerged. Water dribbled in from a plastic pipe that stuck out of the greenery growing in the back wall.

I reckoned the structure had to do with pumping water into the reservoir from an underground stream or something. I didn't know. Whatever it was, it didn't look like it was being used any-more. One of the steel uprights had come away at the top, and brambles had grown nearly right over the top. The whole thing looked like it might be very useful to me.

I'm always careful about getting to the cage. I listen for ages to check that no one can see me leaving. I'm a lot more careful than that stupid fox was. At least my boy isn't roaring anymore. I'm glad. It's a horrible sound. You just want to turn and run. When I'm sure no one is watching me, I step from the path. I weave through the trees and push through the thorn hedge. There's a bit of a gap now, I've come so often. I'm nearly there and I can hear snorting and water splashing. He growls, a low rasping sound that seems to come from the bottom of his guts.

He's smelled me.

I hear him thrashing around in the cage, and a splash of water hits me in the face. I kneel on the concrete and look through the bars. There is the gleam of an eye in the darkness. I have the key to the padlock in my pocket. I feel scared. I can't help it. You would be too. The hatch is on the roof of the cage. He can't get out. But I shiver all the same. Especially now when he has gone quiet and I can't see him. I unlock the padlock and lift the hatch. I drag the pig out of its bag and pull it to the hole. I shove it in, booting the last of it through. The relief is instant but I haven't finished yet. I used to watch him feed. I used to lie on the bars and see him tear the flesh in a frenzy. Now I leave quickly and fetch the other half. I hug the naked, wet flesh in my arms and stagger back to the cage. This half feels heavier. It's probably because I'm tired and because my hand hurts. I rest on the bank next to the cage, holding the pig close to my body. It's still barely recognizable as a pig. In just a few seconds it will be a mess of blood and bone.

I'm tired. I want to be clean. I want to be in my own bed in my own flat, with my own bedding that doesn't stink of the piss and sweat of hundreds of other kids. I want to be holding the warm back of a soft girl.

I unlock the hatch and open it, lowering it gently so it won't clang on the bars. The pig's too heavy. I can't just drop it. My arms won't do it. I push the thing towards the hole and its front dangles into the hatch. I grab the back leg and lower the pig through, inch by inch. Then it feels like the bar is collapsing beneath me and I fall forward. The bloody cage is coming apart! Before I can get my balance there is this incredible yank and I am flipped on my side, my head bashing against the metal. I am dragged towards the hole.

Let go, let go, LET GO.

My arms splay out and catch the sides. My head is sticking out over the hatch, and as the pig hits the water a wall of wet is launched into my face. I throw myself back and slam down the hatch as his jaws smash into the bars beneath me.

FOUR

I don't keep my dad in a cage. What kind of a weirdo do you think I am? I'll tell you what's in there. It's an animal, a bloody monster. You'll see it soon enough, don't worry. I've got my plans.

So I've dispatched the pig and I'm driving back to the house and I'm feeling pretty sketchy. I've got something new to worry about. One of the bars has rusted through and the water cage is no longer secure. It's unlikely he could bust his way out. But the possibility is still there. This situation can't carry on. I mean, I almost died back there. And I'm injured. When I was being dragged over the bars my face got hurt. One of my front teeth got knocked and now it has a horrible tingly feeling. I hope it doesn't fall out. I've got good teeth. They're straight, with no fillings. Everyone's jealous of my teeth. Even Carol told me they were quite good. When I first arrived at the house, three years ago, she was wearing braces. She had one set of wires over the top and another over the bottom. Perhaps this is what made her turn against me; she was jealous of me. But you can't decide to hate someone because you are jealous of their teeth. Can you?

I stop the car and hide the bloodstained pig sack in a hedge because I can't stand the smell of it.

It's about midnight when I arrive home. I hear the hum of the television and go into the sitting room. Jimmy's waiting up for me. He looks pale, and there are deep wrinkles round his eyes.

"I was worried," he says.

I nod.

I can't believe that Jimmy and Verity fell for my story; that my dad was so hungry I was taking him a dead pig. Why didn't they ask me why I didn't take him a packet of club biscuits and some tea bags, like a normal person?

I'll tell you why they didn't question me: It's because they think we're both animals. Oh, yes, Jimmy lets me live in his house and asks me to do the dishes with his daughter. He gives me lifts to town and buys me a CD player at Christmas. But deep down, in his heart, he is frightened of me. I am trouble. And the reason he has me in his house is because he gets paid for it. And so he can tell his friends, "Oh, yes, we take the very worst kids. The ones no one else will have." This makes him feel important. It gives his crummy life meaning. But he thinks I am dangerous. As you have seen, he believes that I am capable of murder. And I can't believe I let him get away with it. Perhaps he felt guilty and that's why he didn't question me too deeply about the pig.

His precious daughter, Carol, is far more capable of murder than me.

Jimmy fiddles with the remote control. This is because he can't look me in the face and needs to have something to do. I might just be paranoid though. Carol says I'm paranoid. I didn't know what it meant when she first called me that. I thought it meant someone disabled. Now I know she's just about right. Anyone would be paranoid with Carol living in the house.

Jimmy has worked out what he wants to say. He twizzles on the sofa to face me. It's a big deal for him, I reckon.

"Stephen," he says, "should we tell Mindy about this?"

"No," I say automatically. Mindy is my social worker, and I learned a long time ago it's best not to tell her anything.

Jimmy is unsurprised. "Hang on. This pig thing. It's pretty extreme. She might be able to get your dad some kind of help. You've got enough to worry about at the moment."

He doesn't need to tell me that. But my dear old dad is the least of my problems. Maybe he can be of use though. After all, he's the one who got me into this mess in the first place. I wonder if I'd be able to find him. It's been what? Two years?

"Mindy's not as bad as you think," says Jimmy.

I give Jimmy a look. "What, do you fancy her or something?" I know this is a stupid thing to say. It's the sort of mouthing off I did a few years ago. But whenever I hear the name *Mindy* I get all worked up and if I think about her enough I feel slightly sick.

Mindy.

She's been my social worker for four years and has only recently learned to spell my first name. And she calls me "Steve."

"How was your father?" asks Jimmy.

"Hungry," I say.

"Is he not collecting his benefits?"

"The unemployment office messed up. He's been short for a few weeks."

I have to admit I'm pretty impressed with myself and I

congratulate myself on my imagination and quick thinking. Maybe there's hope for me after all.

Jimmy feels under a cushion and hands me a brown envelope.

"This came for you this morning," he says.

"It's been opened," I say, looking at it.

"Sorry," Jimmy says. "Carol thought it was for her."

"Why, has she forgotten how to read her own name?" I stomp out of the room and slam the door. I bet everyone in the whole bloody house has read it. I feel a new spike of hatred for Carol. Imagine if I'd done that, read her personal letters. I'd get a bloody lecture about the need for respect and privacy. I bet Carol got off scot-free. I go into my room. I wish I had a lock. Carol and Robert both have locks on their doors. And bolts on the inside. Mind you, these were there before I arrived so I know it wasn't because of me. Like I said before, the Reynoldses like to have the worst kids. I bet Carol and Robert have seen a few things in their time. A few crazies. I knew one kid who came here, a few years before me — Alan Granger. He was a bloody psycho even though he was just this pasty little kid. He smashed up the staff room in the children's home and knifed one of the workers. He got into drugs. I heard he's inside now. He's only two years older than me.

Alan Granger would have slept in my room, in my bed. The thought makes me want to spew. I wonder if he was the one who drew the pictures. I doubt it. He wasn't the type. But you can never tell, can you?

When I first move to a place, I like to see where I am and explore my new territory. I have to check for danger. I can't stand not knowing what's on the other side of the wall. I can't sleep until I've looked in every room. My room is the smallest in the house. It is at the end of a landing. There is a bathroom between me and Robert, then there's Carol's room, then, farthest away from me, Jimmy and Verity. They've got a massive room with bay windows, a dressing room, and an en suite bathroom, all done up in tiny blue shiny tiles. My bedroom isn't so bad. But I can tell hundreds of kids have slept here. There's a certain smell: the smell of urine and fear. A few too many leaky boys have pissed on the carpet. A few too many abandoned kiddies have had a sneaky smoke here. The pillow is limp from nighttime crying sessions. The wallpaper is cheap, nasty woodchip. Down behind the headboard there is a load of graffiti. Someone's scrawled the word CAVE — I suppose it's a band name. I've never heard of them anyway. But the rest of the space behind the bed is covered with drawings, like cartoons. They're all of members of the Reynolds family. As soon as I discovered them, the first night I was here, I found out all I needed to know.

First is Jimmy. He's drawn smiling, but with a big empty circle in his head above his eyes. Verity has two heads. One is a gentle lady with flowing hair and blue eyes; the second is a woman with staring eyes and hair made of snakes. Robert is this little dwarf with a huge knob hanging out of his trousers, tying up a teddy bear by its neck. Carol's drawing is horrible. It's spooky. I don't like to look at it. The artist has got this little girl's face on the body of a spider, with long hairy legs in the center of a web. All around are dead bodies strung up and cocooned, and in the picture she is smiling innocently. You can imagine how freaked out I was when I found these pictures. I tried to tell myself to forget them. I knew that I should give the family a chance. But I couldn't get them out of my mind. The wall is grubby above the headboard. The pictures could have been there for years. Or maybe

27

they were done just before I came. I don't know, but they colored my ideas of what the family was like before I'd hardly had a conversation with them. I don't like the idea that those pictures are right next to my head when I'm sleeping. But I can't move the bed because then the pictures will be seen, and everyone might think I've done them.

I sit on my bed, at the end, away from the headboard, and read the letter. I read it twice. I admit I am quite slow at reading. When you've been in and out of school as much as me, it's hard to find the time to learn. The only person who tried hard with me was Mrs. Denny, my first foster mother. I stayed with her two years, and she helped me with the basics. She made me read these crazy little stories. Now I do all right but I am slow. If I had stayed with Mrs. Denny, maybe I'd be reading Shakespeare and stuff like that now. But that was not to be, and here I am, struggling with a one-page letter from my social worker.

I drop it on the duvet and put my head in my hands.

Four weeks. That's all I have left here. After that they've arranged a place for me at St. Mark's in town. It's this really rough hostel where there are police raids and stabbings. It's only one step from St. Mark's to the streets. In four weeks' time I will be all alone in the world, without even a crazy family to talk to. Okay, the Reynoldses aren't my real family, but at least I have a room, stuff, a space for my car. I have most of my meals cooked for me. There is a cupboard full of food. There is Jimmy, who never says the right thing, but at least he talks to me. I have been here three years. Now I only have four weeks left. I'm seventeen and Social Services says they haven't got any responsibility for me. In just a few weeks I am supposed to know what to do about cooking and taxes and bills and electricity meters and rent and insurance and jobs and benefits and curtains and cleaning fluids and bank accounts.

What do I know? I'm just a kid. Most people my age are leaving school and starting jobs or going to college. They get meals cooked for them and still get treated like children. I know. I've stayed with families like that. I know seventeen-year-olds with nine o'clock curfews who have never had a drink or a cigarette.

But I have another new problem now. The Reynoldses' house is only four miles away from the reservoir. Feeding times are easy. I can go and check up on him and see that he's all right. St. Mark's is in town, and that is twenty miles away. How am I going to be able to get to the reservoir if I don't live nearby and can't afford to keep my car? I can't leave him to starve to death, especially now that there is the possibility he can get out. But what else can I do? Nobody else knows about him.

Nobody except my father.

FIVE

There was this ad in the job center.

Meat Operative required for large local factory. Good stamina and physical strength required. £4.70 per hour. Training given. Successful applicants will be encouraged to apply for their Meat Hygiene Certificate.

I had to take it. I couldn't be homeless and jobless, could I? I don't want to end up on the street with all the other losers from the children's home.

Today is my first day. Marshall's factory is about six miles from the Reynoldses' house. You go through Gruton, past the reservoir, and up towards the moors. It's not far from the disused quarry where Robert is always pestering me to take him swimming. I probably won't. Robert's a crap swimmer.

I drive past the turnoff near Gruton Reservoir and wonder what my Beast is doing. Hopefully keeping his head down and sleeping off his massive pork dinner.

I get to the factory at seven a.m. It's a long gray warehouse-type building right in the middle of nowhere. I meet Naomi, the supervisor. I reckon she's in her sixties. She's got a squat body and acts like she's half asleep. She talks to me like she's bored. She gives me a hairnet, a white mesh trilby hat, a white coat, white Wellies, and thin rubber gloves that smell like condoms. She even makes me wear a beard net! I don't even have a beard, just a bit of stubble. Naomi says if I don't want to wear one, I have to shave every day. I feel like a right tit when I get it all on. You'd laugh your head off if you saw me. When I'm led down into the cutting room, I see everyone is wearing the same getup and I feel a bit better.

The radio's playing Orchard FM and all these huge blokes are singing along and throwing down massive joints of meat on metal tables and cutting them up with long knives. Naomi points to a line of people working at a table and says they're mostly students and that I'll be working with them. It's freezing down here. I wish I'd put another T-shirt on. Naomi says it has to be kept this cold for hygiene reasons.

"You'll get used to it," she says, yawning. "The quicker you work, the warmer you'll be."

No sympathy here, then.

So the butchers are cutting up the meat and passing it along the line to have the fat trimmed off. When they make a bad cut or the meat looks dodgy they throw it in this massive mincing machine. Naomi says my job is to stand at the mouth of the mincer and transfer the goo that comes out into shoebox-size metal tins. The meat is pink like a strawberry milk shake and squeezes out like toothpaste. I have to push the lid down on the boxes to make skewered shish kebabs come out of the holes in the bottom. I give it a go and some of the meat squeezes up over the sides and gets in my gloves and on my sleeves. I even find some in my hair. When I have a tray full of kebabs I go to another table and stab a chunk of lemon on the end of each one. A few people stare at me but no one is really interested. I'm standing next to a huge woman with bare, blotchy arms. She's red-faced and sweaty and I can smell her armpits. I can't believe she's hot. It's freezing in here.

I wish I'd found a different job. The cold is making my tooth tingle.

There's this girl who's in charge of cutting up the lemons. That's what she does all day. She tops and tails the lemons, then cuts them in half and quarters them. Then she brings them over to the line of kebab makers. The girl has very short hair and these big dark eyes. At about eleven o'clock everyone goes off for a break. I follow along and we go up into the daylight. The cutting rooms are all underground. I hadn't realized at first, but when we are sitting in the canteen, the sunlight comes through the windows and I feel the warmth creep up my arms and into my body. I watch the girl. She's sitting with a few other girls but doesn't talk to them much. She drinks coffee from her polystyrene cup and gets a chocolate bar from her pants pocket. The heat from her body must have melted it because she's making a right mess, licking the chocolate from the wrapper and getting it all around her mouth. She sees me watching her and I look away.

At three-thirty all the butchers leave and the place is quiet, without all the singing and shouting and clattering. Someone switches the station to Radio One but it isn't much better. We work for another hour and then all the meat in the mincer runs out. I'm supposed to work until five, but everyone else is leaving and I haven't seen anything of Naomi since lunchtime so I decide to go home too. I'm walking towards the loose plastic strips that hang in the doorway when I notice the massive freezers lining the sides of the walls. I look around and try the lid of the nearest. It's unlocked. Very interesting.

When I was a kid and lived at home, my uncle worked in a slaughterhouse and was always bringing us bags of steaks and joints of pork. He called it a perk of the job.

Outside I just stand for a minute, feeling the rain on my cheek. It's warmer out here and it's March! The air smells really fresh. I get in my car and watch the students climb into a minibus. The girl is with them. I hope that doesn't mean she's a student. I hope she's a dropout like me.

I watch the minibus drive away and I try to work out how much I've earned. My hours are seven-thirty till five — that's nine and a half hours, minus half an hour unpaid lunch break. I wished I'd managed to stay in school longer. Then this sum would be easy. I can't believe the number of child haters who work in schools. I don't know how other kids stick with it. I get there in the end though I run out of fingers very quickly. Forty-two pounds and thirty pence, that's what I've earned today. Kazumba! Petrol money for a fortnight! Two hundred and eleven pounds fifty a week. Times that by five, that makes eight hundred and forty-six pounds a month. I'm going to be bloody rich. I can afford the odd pig on that, and food and rent. I'm not going to be on the street. I'm able to look after myself. The only problem is I have to go back down into that freezing basement for nine hours every day. I don't know if I can do it.

So I'm driving home. It's about five p.m. and I'm knackered and I see an animal lying by the side of the road. I dip my lights in case it's scared, but it doesn't move. I drive past and pull over. I put my emergency lights on so I can see and I get out of the car.

It's a badger and I think it's dead. But it's hard to tell by the red flashing lights. Somebody told me that badgers can bite your hand off. I see a hairy body and teeth. It's not breathing. I cannot bring myself to touch it so I get the car jack from the trunk, and poke it.

"I know someone who would like you," I tell it. I am still scared to touch it with my bare hands but I want to put it in my car. It is too good an opportunity to miss, so I take my sneakers off and put them over my hands. The insides of the sneakers are warm and slightly damp. The trunk is open and I kneel and try to pick up the animal. It's too heavy and the sneakers are useless. I think of how I can't afford any more pigs until I get paid, and I let the shoes fall from my hands and just pick the thing up. It is still warm even though it's a cold night. The hair is thick and wiry and the thing stinks worse than dog shit. It probably has fleas and ticks and God knows what, but I put it in the trunk of my car and slam down the hatch. I wonder how long it will keep. The Beast isn't going to be hungry for a while. Maybe I could freeze it?

Stephen, my boy, I tell myself, *you'll never be able to explain a frozen badger to Verity when she's rummaging for her ice cream.*

I wonder if I should go straight to the reservoir. I would have a hard job explaining a dead badger to Jimmy. My old man is never going to eat that, is he?

I decide to go home. I'm knackered.

At the Reynoldses' house everyone is out except Robert, who is playing his Xbox and eating pizza. I immediately feel more relaxed. I like Robert. He makes me laugh. He's an odd little kid.

"Hey, bro," he says when he sees me. Not one other kid in any of the millions of foster homes I have been in has called me that. Not one. But I have known Robert since he was nine so he has gotten used to me being around. Unlike his sister.

"They've gone to a fucking barn dance!" says Robert.

I like that too. He's this posh middle-class kid who has piano lessons and goes to school every day with a clean shirt, but he swears worse than the butchers in the meat factory. I've been tempted to tell Robert about the reservoir and the cage and the pigs. But I can't; he is after all one of the Reynolds family. He belongs to them, not me. And to be honest, if I did show him, I have no idea how he would react. This is part of why I like him. He's unpredictable. A wild card. Sometimes he has lots to tell me, other days he doesn't. He never pretends to be in a good mood when he isn't. Sometimes he reminds me of Selby.

I'm not really a snooper, but I like to know what's going on around me. And I happen to know that Robert's bedroom walls are plastered with pictures of naked women. He's only eleven! There's nothing too rude, just tits and bums and lots of hair. And you really wouldn't want to look under the bed. I mean, where does a kid like Robert get this stuff from? Jimmy doesn't have anything like it, at least not that I've found. I can't imagine my gran putting up with that sort of thing. I'd be too embarrassed to have stuff like that, let alone display it on the wall.

"Has Carol gone with them?" I ask. I always like to know the position of the enemy.

"She's gone out to one of her mates'," says Robert. "Give me a cigarette, will you?"

I tut. "Your mum wouldn't like it."

"Oh, don't be so tight." He holds out his hand. "I need one so I can concentrate on my homework."

I give in. I'm a bit of a soft touch when people are being nice to me.

"All right," I say. "But smoke it outside and throw the butt in the bin." I fish a cigarette out for him and he wrinkles up his face in disgust.

"Low tar, you stingy minger." But he takes it anyway.

I make myself a sandwich and decide that I might as well take the badger to the reservoir tonight, seeing as everyone is out. I have this idea that the more I stuff him with meat, the quieter he'll be. I admit I am feeling nervous. God knows what my little pet would have done to me if he'd dragged me into that cage. That's all the thanks I get for looking after him for over six years. I look outside to the porch where Robert is smoking the cigarette right down to the filter. I want to warn him not to burn his fingers. He is nothing like my other brother, Chas, though they are about the same age. Chas is in another foster home. He's been there nearly a year now. I've only seen him once since he moved in. Maybe I should phone him, but that would mean I'd have to get the number off Mindy and I'm not talking to that cow if I can help it. Chas is a sweet little kid. People always want to look after him. My gran was mad when they took him away. She said they were denying her human rights but they said they couldn't risk it. It's because my mum lives with her and she's not a very good mother. I won't go into that now. The only other thing I'll say about my mum is that she did try to look after us. (Unlike my dear father.) But some people, like my parents, shouldn't have kids. There are three of us. Selby, me, and Chas. Things got messy. My mum couldn't cope — well, she never could, really. She's not like other people's mothers. For one thing, she shaves her head, even though she says she hates it. Like I said. I'll leave it there for now. I need to think about the badger I've got in the back of my car and how I'm going to get it through the hatch without any trouble.

So I'm driving up to the lake. It's really dark now, about nine p.m., and I see something scamper in the headlights. Everything is out on the roads tonight. I don't know what comes over me but instead of slamming on the brakes I put my foot down and swerve towards it. I want to hit it, whatever it is. I'm on a feeding frenzy for my boy. I'm going to stuff him so full of meat he's going to keep quiet for a month. Whatever this thing is, I'm going to mow it down and use it as food. If my boy isn't hungry, he's less likely to try to escape. It's like the devil has grabbed hold of my hands and is steering towards these bright, unblinking eyes in the road.

There's a knock from the front right wheel and I stop the car. I sit for a moment or two. What have I done? I'm a murderer. I deliberately set out to kill something. And it wasn't a pheasant or anything little like that. It was something bigger. Something that

I thought would keep my boy quiet for a bit. Something to settle his scaly old stomach. What the hell did I do that for? I open the door and get out. It feels like I have finally turned bad. I am like one of the psycho kids in the home. The really messed-up ones, like Alan Granger. The inside of my head is black.

I wonder if this is the beginning of a new me. A me who will end up in the nick. A me who does terrible things.

I look under the wheel. It's not a hare or another badger or a fox. It's a small dog.

And it's still breathing.

SIX

"You can't keep him, I'm afraid," says Verity. She wipes the bread crumbs from the table and holds them in her fist. She looks tired and her eye makeup is smeared down one cheek. This barn dancing must be hot stuff.

"Why not?" I ask, though I know the answer. "Carol's got her cat, you've got Robert. Why can't I have a pet?"

"Oh, Stephen," she says, and gives me the famous Verity Look. It is intended to silence me and make me see sense. But I'm not letting her off that easily. I know I can't have a pet because I'm not going to be here much longer. But I want her to say that. To spell it out to me.

"We'll take him to the RSPCA tomorrow," she says. "He's a nice little dog. Someone will give him a good home. The owner might even come forward."

"He's a stray," I say. "Look at him."

The dog looks like a cross between a whippet and a Staffordshire bull terrier. He has these big wet eyes and a square body. He has a bald patch on his knee and his head. He's so thin you can see his ribs, and when he did a turd in the garden there were tiny white worms wriggling in it. He has a cut on his back where the car hit him. Other than that he's fine.

"Malackie," I say. "I'm going to call him Malackie." (I heard one of the meat cutters going on about some guy called Malackie. I liked the name.)

"Oh, Stephen," sighs Verity. "Don't get attached."

Story of my life.

Malackie and I walk out.

I don't go to work the next day. I wonder if I'll get the sack but frankly I don't care. I'll get another job. It didn't seem so bad when I was there but now it seems the factory is rank. I don't know if I'm going to be able to eat meat again for a long time.

Malackie and I drive out to the reservoir. A tractor pulls in to let us pass and I stick my thumb up at the driver. He's about my age. I wish I was him. Driving my daddy's huge tractor around and milking cows and lambing sheep and cutting corn. Going on Young Farmers' piss-ups and having my life all mapped out for me. That kid isn't due to be kicked out of his foster home and end up at a dodgy hostel with junkies and tramps.

I stop in the pull-off near the reservoir and take the badger out of the trunk and dump it on the verge. Malackie sniffs it and backs away.

"You're right, boy," I say. "I shouldn't feed him that. It's not fit for anything to eat. But I haven't got any choice, have I?"

I wrap the badger in a couple of trash bags to carry it to the water. I've tied a rope to Malackie's collar and wrapped it around my wrist. He trots behind me like he's known me forever. He digs his paws into me when I carry him up over the fence. Maybe he's scared I'm going to drop him over like I did with the badger. We're getting close now. Malackie stops to pee on a clump of nettles and I put the sack down and give my arms a rest. The dog sniffs the bag again and gives me a weird look.

When I'm sure nobody is around, I step from the path.

As we approach the cage I hear splashing. I hope he doesn't make a noise when he smells me coming. It's too risky. Malackie won't go near the cage no matter how hard I drag him. He sits down, digs his back legs in the ground, and puts his tail between his legs. I tie him to a branch and creep closer. I peer through the bars. I see nothing but manky water, but I know he's there, waiting for me.

I used to lie on the bars at dusk and watch him, a dark shape in the water. When he was smaller he swam around his cage. Now he is so big he lies just beneath the surface and watches me watching him. Sometimes he sinks to the bottom. Just like that. One minute he's there, the next he's gone. One night I watched him climb out of the water and halfway up the bars. He clawed all around the walls of the cage, thrashing and roaring. I sat a long way off. Even then I was nervous, like part of him could reach out and flick me through the bars down into the water below.

There's a commotion in the cage and I see flapping wings. A pigeon beats against the bars. How did it get in? I watch it for a minute. *Come on, Stephen*, I tell myself. *Get on with it*. I scramble up the bank, dragging the badger behind me. Willing myself not to look down, I drop to my knees and crawl onto the barred roof of the cage with the badger balanced over my shoulder. The dead animal stinks, and I imagine insects crawling out of it into my ears. I make sure I spread my weight evenly over several bars and avoid the broken one. It's much slower this way, and I have this fear that more bars will collapse. I unlock the hatch. I'm shaky. I can see where the broken strut has rusted through. It's bent down into the cage. If I put any weight on it I'll tumble into the water. I stop for a minute to try to slow my breathing. If I'm quiet, maybe he'll stay where he is and not lunge for me. He's grown so huge, he might be able to stick his head right out of the hatch. How am I to know? I can't see him properly. Maybe the pigeon will distract him. I feel more confident in the daylight, but as I open the hatch, I lose my nerve and kick the dead badger in, sack and all. It falls into the water and sinks. I push back the hatch and wait for the carnage. There is an eerie silence, then Malackie lets out a whine.

"Shhh," I say. "You're next." I swear the dog gives me a dirty look. "Only joking," I say. The bird settles on the ledge and begins preening itself. Suddenly my boy surfaces. One greeny eye watches me and his mouth is pulled into a horrible kind of grin. I blink in shock. I know he's gotten big, but this is ridiculous. He must be nearly twelve or thirteen feet long. It must be all those pigs. But if I feed him less, he'll be more dangerous because he'll be hungry. To my horror the pigeon flaps up and perches on his head. I see the shine in his eye. I know what he can do to a pig in a matter of seconds. But there's no massacre. The bird walks with skinny legs along the scaly head. Maybe they've made friends.

"Cool," I say. "I got Malackie and you got the pigeon."

I eyeball my Beast.

"What am I going to do with you?" I mutter. I stand there, weighing my options.

Some of them aren't very nice. Not very nice at all.

The bird flaps off to the side as the head submerges. The sack has been floating, the badger half-in and half-out of it. I can see one of its paws. All the hairs splay out. Then it's gone, pulled underwater. There is nothing except a swirl of water that slowly turns pinky red. I step back. I untie Malackie and we head back towards the car. I worry about the pigeon. I should have left the hatch open for a few minutes to give the poor thing a chance. I ought to go back. But I can't. I just want to get away.

Back on the path I see a man walking towards me. He's pretty fat with a snubby nose. He's seen me and there's nowhere to run. He looks annoyed. I recognize him though I've only seen him once before, in the parking lot in his van a couple of years ago. I remember the van had BEXTON WATER AUTHORITY written on the side in swirly white letters. I decide he's got something to do with working the dam. But what's he doing out here? The dam is about half an hour's walk away.

"No dogs allowed, son," he says. He has a wrinkled brown face and big shoulders. But what I notice most of all is this necklace he's wearing. It's a tooth on a chain. A long, pointy, sharp tooth. I must look shocked because he suddenly looks more friendly and goes on about farmers and insurance and dogs worrying sheep.

I nod and make to move on, but he holds out his hand.

"I see you here quite often," he says. "Live round here, do you?"

"Sort of," I say.

"Where?"

"Down the village."

"What's your name?"

I don't miss a beat. "Danny Slater."

Maybe he knows about my pet. Maybe he knows I feed it. He could just be playing me along. I can't take my eyes off that tooth. He has bored a hole in it and the silver chain is threaded through.

The man eyes me up for a few seconds.

"Don't bring the dog here," he says. "And you don't ever swim here, do you?"

"No," I say. I haven't swum in the reservoir since I brought my Beast here.

"There's dangerous currents," says the bloke. "Especially near the dam. And the mud is deep. It can pull you under." He steps closer. "And you have to remember this is drinking water. This is what comes out of your taps and what your mum cooks your potatoes in."

"Right," I say. I'm about to walk off when I do something stupid. I open my big mouth.

"Where did you get that?" I point at the necklace.

The Dam Man fingers it.

"I found it on the shoreline a few years ago," he says, "just below here." He points in the direction of the water cage. "Crazy, huh? No one knows what it is. I reckon it's a tusk from a pig."

On the shoreline! There's a flow of water from the cage where it pours out of a hole in the concrete down into this over-grown channel and into the reservoir. It's possible that my boy could have lost a tooth, and it was swept down by the current. But it should have sunk in the mud at the bottom of the lake.

I nod at the bloke, tug on Malackie's rope, and walk on. After a few paces I glance back at the bloke. He's going off the path towards the water cage!

"Oh, shit," I say. When he's out of sight I double back and follow him.

He walks down through the undergrowth where I've just been and stares at the gap in the thorn hedge.

I find myself a vantage point in some dead bracken behind a tree and watch. I hug Malackie tightly to me. I can hardly breathe.

Does this man know?

The man takes a paper out of his pocket, unfolds it, and studies it. He's looking for something. To my alarm, he pushes himself through the thorns.

I ought to run off now, but I can't. I have to see this. I have to follow.

"Ah," says the Dam Man. He's seen the overgrown cage.

He walks round the cage and tugs at one of the bars. I can't hear any sound from the water. If he finds my little pet, he'll remember me and think I'm involved. Oh, God. He's climbing up the bank. He's going to see him. It's all over. I crush Malackie's ear in my fingers before realizing what I am doing, and he lets out a little whimper. The Dam Man stops and looks hard in our direction. I freeze and hold Malackie tightly. I slowly let out my breath as the man moves again.

"Sorry, boy," I whisper, unable to take my eyes away from the man.

He looks at the cage, testing all the bars on the roof with his foot. He finds the damaged ones and balances along the metal bars to examine the hatch. I hear him muttering to himself. I hope he doesn't attract my boy's attention. Oh, no. He's noticed something. He's looking right down into the cage.

"What?" says the man.

There's a fluttering noise as a pair of wings bash against the bars.

"How did you get in here?" The Dam Man lifts the padlock. "I haven't got a key, mate. You'll have to get out the same way you got in."

Don't look down.

I picture the floating eyes staring up at the bloke's meaty body.

But he's coming down. I can't believe it. He hasn't seen him. He stands on the grass, leaning on the cage, stretches his arms over his head, and lets out a loud belch. I imagine a dark shape looming up behind him and a jaw pushing through the bars and teeth puncturing his jacket. But there's no roar, no splashing. It's as if there is nothing in the cage except an old pigeon and a pit of water. The bloke starts walking towards me and I turn and run, dragging Malackie after me by the collar.

Malackie is pleased to see the car (which is a surprise because it nearly killed him yesterday) and he jumps into the passenger seat, wagging his tail. I stroke his head and he thumps his tail. I switch on the ignition and we drive off.

But I'm not going to the factory, and I'm not going back to the Reynoldses'. Not yet. It's only the middle of the day. I've got to sort things out. I'm off on my mission impossible.

After about five miles the landscape changes. We climb up to the moors, where the trees are all stunted by the wind and heather grows by the side of the road. We pass a load of little ponies who carry on munching even as we burn by. I turn off down a tiny lane and it's all potholed and rough with grass growing down it like a Mohawk haircut.

I take my rucksack and Malackie and leave my car pulled up on the verge. I climb over a gate and follow a stony path up to the top. It's cold, and I pull my hat low over my head. I can see for miles. I look down at a forest ahead; staring at the tops of the trees till my eyes are watering, I wonder if this is going to be a waste of time. Malackie pulls at his rope and barks at the wind.

"Good boy," I say, and he gives me a dog grin. I'm glad he's too thick to realize I tried to kill him. We follow a path down towards the forest. I can't stop thinking about what happened this morning. I can't understand how the Dam Man didn't see anything. Maybe it's because he smells different than me, so the Beast stayed quiet. Or maybe my boy was there all along, lying on the bottom, and the inspector bloke never noticed him. The man didn't expect there to be anything there, so there wasn't. And the water was probably murky after the pig and the badger, so maybe he couldn't see the bottom. Whatever the reason, I've had a lucky escape. If the Dam Man had discovered my Beast, the place would now be crawling with police and reporters. They'd all want to know how he got there. The Dam Man would remember me, and that would be it. I'd be famous. It might be quite good. I might make some money out of it. But life is not like that. They'd either kill my boy or put him in a manky zoo and throw me in the nick for owning a dangerous animal without a license.

I push away the brambles and step into a clearing. Several large trees lie uprooted, and grasses and reeds grow to my waist. This is mad. I'm probably coming out all this way on a wild-goose chase. Something squeals in the trees and the branches sway. I glimpse a hairy tail and bright, rodent eyes. It's a squirrel, and Malackie wants to chase it. I should let him off the lead but he might never come back. Geese fly over the treetops. I look at the leader, flying at the apex of the V. Somebody told me that the one that flies in front has to work hardest, and when it gets tired it falls back and another takes its place. Responsibility for navigation is shared among the strongest birds, and the older and weaker they become, the farther back in the V they fly.

I find a rabbit with dusty eyes lying dead in a snare. The fur is dewy and a trickle of blood drips out of its nostrils. This is a good sign. Maybe I'll be in luck after all. I take the wire off the rabbit's neck and pick up the floppy body. I put it in my rucksack. It will be handy later. I should get an award for Most Imaginative Ways to Feed Your Pet. No one can say I don't try.

I climb a steep bank, pulling myself up on the trees. My sneakers are stuck with pine needles. Every so often a tree is marked with a dab of orange paint. I think this means it's going to be cut down. Someone has been here recently. I see a Coke can and a faded bag of chips. A candy wrapper lies half buried in needles. The ground is soft, and I wonder if I'm smelling smoke. I stop. Strung between two trees is a dark, sagging hammock, and a plume of smoke comes out over the leaves. It crosses my mind that I should turn and quietly walk away.

But the bundle in the hammock stirs, sensing my presence. I see a mop of hair and a brown hand with broken, dirty, crusted nails.

"Dad," I say.

SEVEN

Six years ago, when I was just eleven, me and Selby climbed up onto the roofs off High Street. It was really early in the morning, about seven o'clock. Selby took me over all these roofs until we came to a wall that looked down on the prison gates. We were nearly level with the high prison wall, and there was a big clock like Big Ben striking out the hour. Selby pointed at a wooden door in the redbrick wall and a man came out. He looked a bit dazed. It was a bright morning and we had the sun behind us, but I was worried he would see us, so I ducked behind the wall. Selby told me not to be so soft. All the same, when I looked again, I could only bring myself to look at his shadow at first. It was long and slanted and carried a big bag.

The man paused and looked around him, like he was seeing everything for the first time. Even from a distance I could see that the suit didn't fit him properly and his shoes were black and shiny.

"That can't be him, Selb," I whispered.

Selby jabbed me in the ribs. "'Course it is. Look at him." He fished a pair of binoculars out of his pocket, a pair he'd nicked from the market. He adjusted the eyepieces and handed them to me. I looked through and followed the red bricks down till I reached the man.

"Yeah," I said, feeling weird. "It's him." He had dark hair like mine, and pale skin. His shoulders were the same shape as Selby's.

It was our dad all right. He'd been in the nick for three whole years. And I hadn't seen him once. He'd gone down for violent burglary. Selby said it must have been pretty bad to get three years without parole.

"Give them to me." Selby snatched the binoculars as my dad walked off.

We followed him, crawling up roofs and sliding down walls. Selby found a fire escape and we climbed down to the road. We hid behind parked cars and trees and Dumpsters. It was quite exciting. We always kept our distance.

Dad crossed the road and stopped at a bus shelter. He put his bag on the pavement and watched the seagulls screeching overhead.

"He looks stoned," I whispered from behind a Mazda on the other side of the road.

"Probably is," said Selby.

"Reckon he'll go to Gran's?" I asked.

Selby shrugged.

Just then a bus drew up. Our dad was the only one waiting, but as he went to get on he turned his head back in our direction. I couldn't move. I just thought what a funny sight we must look, two skinny heads peeking over the hood of the car. I don't know what I expected back then. Definitely not some soppy reunion.

Not my dad dropping his bags and running over to us, saying, "My sons," and taking us off for a big slap-up breakfast somewhere. It was a good thing I didn't expect that.

My dad saw us. I know that. Something crossed over his face but I can't really explain it. He stared for a few seconds, then gave himself a little shake and got on the bus. My mouth fell open.

As the bus drove past, he looked out the window at us, then turned his head away. Then the bus was gone.

"Bastard," said Selby.

He didn't go to Gran's.

The man in the hammock, my father, sits up.

"It's you," he says in his best rasping voice.

I nod.

"What do you want?"

My dad's never been one to roll out the red carpet. The first time me and Selby found him out here, he tried to chase us off.

"Got a smoke?" he asks now.

I give him two. At least he has his own lighter. Everyone's bumming cigarettes off me these days.

My dad lives in a wood in a steep valley right in the middle of the moors. At least sometimes he lives here. In winter he's usually hanging around the hostels in town. I thought I might find him here because it's nearly spring. He has this hut, made of planks and a tarpaulin, with a stove in it. Outside he has another fire and his hammock. There's an old trash can he uses to collect rainwater. He has a kettle and pots and pans sitting under a gorse bush. There are food wrappings and scraps of plastic lying everywhere. A white raggedy sheet hangs in the branches like Dad was trying to build something and gave up. I'm standing on cigarette butts, dead leaves, and a rotting item of clothing. Dad's made a right mess. Empty milk cartons lie around alongside half-buried planks and scraps of metal. The only thing that looks organized is a massive woodpile close to the hut. There's a sharp saw on a wide log. Malackie sniffs at the woodpile and cocks his leg.

"Any grub?" my dad asks. I think of the pig and fight a crazy urge to laugh.

I hand him a banana, three oranges, and six apples, all nicked from the Reynoldses' everlasting fruit bowl. My dad looks disappointed. "Nothing else?" he asks. "A drink?"

I shake my head. I'm not giving him the rabbit. I'm keeping that for somebody else.

My dad swings his legs round and sits up. He runs his hand through his mop of hair. His beard has gotten bigger. It's all dark and matted and streaked with gray. His hair is clumping into a massive dreadlock on the back of his head. His hands are as filthy as his nails. His skin is tanned a deep brown and there's a smear on his nose. He's wearing a torn pair of pants and a thick winter coat. He smells of pee and smoke and BO. I look closer at his boots. They're brand-new Caterpillars.

"Where did you get those?" I ask.

"Mate gave them to me."

Whenever my dad says his mate has given him something, I know it means he's nicked it.

Dad rubs his eyes, belches, and looks at me. "You here alone?"

"I drove here," I say. "I need a favor."

"Oh, come on, Stephen." Dad finishes the first cigarette and lights up the second.

He's always smoked, my dad. When I think of him I always picture him with a cigarette in his mouth. When he got sent down, when I was about eight years old, there was a smell of smoke around my gran's house for months after he'd gone.

"In trouble, are you?" asks my dad. "You can't stay here."

"It's nothing like that," I say. I'm nervous. My dad has this way about him. You just want to run off and leave him alone. It feels like it wouldn't take much to tip him over the edge. But I hold my ground. After all, he got me into this mess in the first place.

"What else have you got in your bag?" he asks.

"Nothing," I say. But before I can stop him he's grabbed my bag off my shoulder and is rifling through. I feel angry. I mean, I'm not a little kid anymore.

"That's mine," he says, pulling out the rabbit. He gives me a look. "What do you want that for?"

I don't reply. I just get more and more angry watching him pick through my stuff. He finds some coins and asks me if he can have them.

"Please, Stephen — I don't get paid till next week."

Paid! I like that. That's what my dad calls his dole money. He goes to the post office once a fortnight for his check. After my dad left prison, Selby and I traced him to the hostel in town. St. Mark's. That's right; you *have* heard the name before. Nice, eh? You can understand why I'm not keen to go there, not if it accepts scumbags like my dad. In the past I would have let my dad take the money. But not today. He has about three quid in his palm. I had to work in the meat factory to earn that.

"Give it back," I say, and snatch it out of his hand.

My dad is surprised. "No offense, lad. I just thought you might want to help your old dad out."

I always felt like a skinny midget next to him. He makes everyone feel like this. But I am pleased to notice that I am now as tall as him. Soon he won't dare boss me around anymore.

I think he might have noticed I've grown as well, because he gives me back my bag, though he keeps the rabbit. Sitting back on his hammock, he swings gently back and forth on his toes. I try to think what this reminds me of.

"What's this, then? Got some girl in trouble?"

I wish.

"It's two things, actually," I say. I pull on the lead and pull Malackie forward. "I need you to look after my dog. They won't let me keep him."

My father grunts and lies back in his hammock.

"Can't feed him," he says. "I can't feed myself. And I don't want it crapping everywhere."

"Please, Dad."

I don't know why I bother with that. Pleases and thank-yous never make much of an impact on my father.

"No way. Why don't you just leave him at some farm?"

I feel really angry then. It sort of reminds me of how he treated us kids.

"I'm being kicked out of the Reynoldses'," I say. "They're putting me in the hostel."

My father sniffs and looks at me. "Stay off the scag and you'll be all right."

If people had to be interviewed before they became parents, my dad definitely wouldn't have gotten the job.

I lean against a tree and my heel crunches a beer can into the ground. My dad isn't like one of those survival experts you see on the telly. You know the ones, who can make a fire with two bits of wood and eat roasted squirrels. They build fancy shelters and carve spoons out of branches. You'd think he'd know a thing or two about survival because he used to be in the army. But he isn't a hero. He went off to the Gulf, but all he did was fix the trucks and tanks the real soldiers were driving. No, my dad is a messy old man who couldn't survive without his check and the generosity of his "mates."

I'm not going to end up like him.

"Remember that pet you bought me for my birthday when I was a kid?" I say.

He frowns and combs dirty fingers through his beard.

"What, is it him?" He points at Malackie, who is sniffing the hut.

"No, Dad, the one you said you got from Fraser's uncle."

My dad still doesn't get it.

"Off the boats in Cornwall?" I say.

My dad's face lights up.

"We had the three of them off the *Lady Margaret*. My contact wouldn't pay for the third. Said it looked half dead. Evil little thing nearly took my finger off. Didn't you keep it in a fish tank, Stephen?"

I look at my father. His coat has torn away from his forearm and the skin is all purply and wrinkled. How is this useless old drunk going to help me? Then I remember I don't have anyone else to ask.

"Dad, I've still got it."

That makes him look at me. He gives a low whistle and stands up.

"I'd have thought you would have flushed it down the crapper years ago."

"No, Dad," I say.

He looks at me a long while. I recognize something of Selby in his eyes. I don't like this. I'd rather not see any connection to him at all.

"Liar," says my father. "Get out of there, dog." He yanks at the trailing lead as Malackie sniffs inside the hut.

"He's massive," I say. "I've got him caught in this water cage, a sort of pump house. He could escape any day."

"Where?" Dad wipes his nose on his sleeve. He still sounds like he doesn't believe me.

"At the reservoir at Gruton."

I've finally said it. I've kept this a secret for four years. He wasn't so big then, only about three feet long, though he could still inflict some damage. He's maybe four times that now. I finger the scar on my arm.

"I can't look after him anymore," I say. "I've got to get rid of him. I can't afford the meat, and I'm moving soon."

My dad has a funny expression on his face. His mouth is closed tight and he has wrinkled up his eyes like he's staring at the sun. To be crude, he looks like he's having a shit.

"So what do you think I can do?" he asks. "Fly it to the swamps?"

I bite my lip. I have spent a long time thinking about this.

"I want you to help me kill it," I say.

It's the only way I know I'll be free of him. I spend hours at night lying awake and wondering how I can do it. I can't stab the thing — it would just eat me as soon as I got close enough. And I can't poison it. I saw a rat dying of poison once. It was on the grounds of the children's home and was all green-frothing at the mouth and making horrible noises. I just stood and watched. I was only a little kid. I can't do that to an animal no matter how mean it is. Besides, how would I get the dosage right, and how would I get him to eat it?

"Just leave it there," says my dad. "And it will die of starvation."

"But he makes a noise when he gets hungry," I say. "Someone might find him, someone might get killed." I stop there. I'm not going to tell my dad about my dreams, my nightmares, where he breaks out of the cage and goes on a rampage. How even now, if I hear a noise downstairs in the night, if I'm half asleep, I think maybe possibly he's followed my scent back the Reynoldses' house and is waiting for me. I can't tell my dad that I can't go swimming anywhere, in case he's broken out and is hiding underwater. I can't tell him that I've had dreams where Chas, my little brother, is being eaten alive and screaming for help.

"I need a gun," I say.

A gun is definitely the best bet. A clean shot between the eyes and all my troubles will be over.

My dad is quiet for a long time. I had to come here. He's the only person I know who can get me a gun. He must have contacts from his prison days. And having been in the army, he'd know how to work one.

"How old are you now?" asks my dad.

"Eighteen," I lie.

"No way."

I don't know if he is referring to my age or to the possibility of getting me a gun.

"I don't know what else to do," I admit. "He's bloody huge, lethal. You should see him."

My father unscrews the lid of a brown bottle and takes a swig. He chokes a little on the liquid and I watch dribble run over his beard. My father is disgusting. That's not beer he's drinking, it's something really rank, like paraffin.

So he'll probably die soon.

"I'm not getting you a gun, you crazy little shit," he says.

That's what I like, a nice bit of parental support.

"Just leave it to die," he says. "Forget about it." He rolls himself back into his hammock. "Now clear off."

"Dad."

He waves his hand in dismissal.

"He's too dangerous," I say.

"Then take it to the zoo. I don't care. It's nothing to do with me." He turns his back to me.

"You got him for me," I say.

"Bugger off, Stephen."

Something in his voice has changed. It's even thicker, with a kind of growl. As I'm walking away with Malackie, I hear a shout.

"Leave the dog."

EIGHT

I'm not surprised my father refused to help me. He's that sort of bloke. But now I'm stuffed.

I expect you're wondering how I got the thing to the cage in the first place. It wasn't easy, let me tell you. But it was four years ago and he was much, much smaller than he is now. It was before I was staying with the Reynoldses. It was a coincidence that I was moved so close to the reservoir a year later.

I was only thirteen then, but I was quite strong. That's the one thing I'm lucky in: my size. I've always been big for my age. When I was thirteen I was tougher than a lot of sixteen-year-olds. No bullshit. It's true. Anyway, one night I nicked a car from the Lidl parking lot. It was a Volvo Estate. It was definitely not the usual sort of car I went in for. But I needed to keep a low profile. I remember driving like a granny through town to the place where I was keeping him. He was in this bath in my dad's lockup. My dad was in the nick at the time. He'd messed up my mum a bit too badly and even she couldn't disguise it. Not that time.

I had a rope, and I managed to get on his back and hold his mouth shut. Like I said, he was smaller then, about the size of a full-grown collie dog. But he still managed to rip my arm. I couldn't do anything about it. That's what the scar on my arm is all about. I tied up his mouth, wrapped him in a sheet, and carried him down to the Volvo.

I always do things on my own. Even Selby didn't know about my little pet. I couldn't trust Selby. In some ways he's like Robert. Unpredictable. For all I knew Selby would have set the animal on one of his enemies, or something like that. He can do a lot of damage if he puts his mind to it.

I drove out to the reservoir. I didn't know about the pull-off then, so I parked in the parking lot. He was grunting and wriggling in the trunk. I emptied a can of Coke over him because I thought I had better keep him wet, but he didn't seem to like that. I picked him up and he thrashed around a bit, but he couldn't do much because I had tied him up so tightly. He was bloody heavy even then. I carried him along the path until I reached the water cage.

I undid the ropes that held his legs against his body. I admit I wasn't sure how to loosen the ropes that went round his jaws. Don't forget, I was only thirteen. I know kids who are scared of piddly little spiders. I was faced with a squirming, crazy animal with twenty times as many teeth as me! I probably hurt him when I dropped him in the water because I ended up dangling him by the rope that held his jaws shut. Then I got out a bread knife from my bag and hacked at the ropes. There was a bit of string trailing from his jaw for about two years after that. I had no way of getting it off. It didn't seem to do him any harm.

I fitted a new padlock on the hatch. There are three keys.

One is hidden under a nearby stone. The other I keep in my bedroom in my sock drawer. The last I keep on me at all times.

I liked him at first. I liked the mean look of him. I liked the fact he was my secret. I fed him tins of dog food and packets of bacon. I nicked quite a lot of this stuff, but I was also spending most of my money on feeding him. But like you know, as time has gone by he's been eating more and more.

"You've had two telephone calls," Jimmy says, when I arrive back at the Reynoldses' after visiting my dad. "The first was from your supervisor wanting to know why you didn't turn up at work." He raises his eyebrow. "I told her you had flu but should be in tomorrow."

Was that nice of him or not? Is he so desperate to get me out of the house that he'll lie for me?

"I know things are tough for you at the moment," he says.

I shrug and help myself to four cookies from the packet on the kitchen counter. There's a chicken roasting in the oven and pans of vegetables boiling on the cooker.

"What was the other call?" I ask, opening all the sauce-pan lids.

"Mindy. She wants you to attend a review meeting next week to plan your next move."

My next move. When I am kicked out and left to rot in St. Mark's. When I join the rest of the losers. When I'll have to sleep with a knife under my pillow.

"Cheer up," says Jimmy. "Everything will be okay. You're a sensible lad."

At that moment Carol flounces in. She stinks of perfume and is wearing a skirt so short I can practically see the bottom of her arse.

"Darling," says Jimmy, "you forgot to put on your trousers."

"Hardy-har," she says. She focuses on me. "Skiver," she says. "I knew you wouldn't stick that job."

"I'm going in tomorrow," I say.

Carol waitresses in this pub down the road, The Globe, a few times a week. She gets all done up in black and white and comes home with roast potatoes and chocolate flakes nicked from the kitchens.

I tried for a job there, but they wouldn't take me. I really can't think why.

Jimmy slips me a fiver. "For petrol," he says.

Carol looks put out. "Where's mine?"

For once Jimmy ignores her.

"Just try it for a week or so," he says. I assume he is talking about my glamorous job. "It's bound to get better as you settle in, and you might make some friends."

"I doubt that," mutters Carol.

Sometimes when I look at Carol I get this feeling like I could just grab her, take her throat in my hands, and slowly, slowly squeeze, pushing down on her windpipe. I have this feeling now. I think Carol notices because she skips off.

"Have you gotten her a card?" whispers Jimmy.

"What?" I struggle to bring myself out of my murderous thoughts.

"It's her birthday tomorrow. Remember?"

I shake my head. I couldn't care less.

62

"Verity's bought one for you to sign, just in case. It's in the sideboard."

I help myself to another cookie.

Carol's going to be sixteen. Sweet sixteen. What a laugh that is. Sick sixteen is more like it.

"You seem a bit glum," says Jimmy.

Glum! What kind of a lamby word is that? I shake my head. "I'm fine," I say.

I mean, I can hardly admit that I'm pissed off because my ex-con dad has refused to get me a gun so I can do a killing, can I?

"Where's the dog?" asks Jimmy.

"I gave it to my dad," I say. It feels strange telling the truth, like sucking lemons.

Jimmy looks surprised. "Is that where you've been today?"

I nod. All this truth-telling makes me feel weak, so I sit down.

"How is he?"

"He's a scabby old man," I say slowly.

Jimmy sighs. "I wish we could have let you keep the dog, Stephen. But you know it's not practical at the moment." He draws up a chair and sits down. "I think you need some fun in your life."

I give him a look. The sort of fun I like isn't legal.

"I appreciate things are tough, what with moving out and your dad and everything."

"I'm not going to St. Mark's," I say.

Jimmy nods. "It's not ideal, is it? Mindy says she's trying to get you in supported lodging."

"Yeah, right." I think what I say next is because I'm fed up with all of them pretending to care about me when really they don't. "I'm going to my gran's," I say with a sidelong glance. "Back to my real family."

Jimmy looks worried. He fiddles with a mug Carol has left on the table.

"Are you sure that's a good idea, with your mum being there and everything?"

I face him. "It's better than St. Mark's."

Jimmy nods. "It probably is. Have you spoken to your gran about this? I had no idea."

"Course I have," I lie. "So tell Mindy she doesn't have to bother."

"You can tell her yourself at your review meeting next week," says Jimmy.

I hate review meetings. They take up approximately one and a half hours of my life, every six months. Jimmy and Verity are there, also Mindy, her boss, and the latest support worker or mentor or whoever they've dragged up who is supposed to have some interest in my well-being. They never invite my gran. Then they sit and patronize me. When I was younger I'd be a real pain in the arse. I'd refuse to say anything, or try to get my foster parents into trouble, or just walk out. It was fun to see these big shots from Social Services, with all their university degrees and diplomas and political correctness, get mad when I ripped up a form or spat on the carpet. I have to admit that it gave me the greatest pleasure. I love watching those sorts of people lose control. It's funny. They think they're better than us, but they get wound up over the tiniest things. It's irresistible.

I don't mess around these days. I just sit. I used to think if I cooperated, then the meeting would be over quicker. But oh, no. This lot will always find something else to talk about. So I just sit and take it. Like going to the dentist. And when it's over, normal life doesn't seem quite so bad. I mean, what could be worse than having a group of strangers, who claim to know you, who have read your files and know that your dad is violent and your mum is a nutter, talk over your head about "stimulation" and "career pathways?"

I can just picture the scene:

Mindy: *So, Steve, is there anything worrying you?*
Me: *Yeah, you lot are about to throw me out on the street, without any money, after dragging me away from my family when I was a kid.*
Mindy: *And how does that make you feel?*
Me: *That you useless bastards have messed up my life.*
Mindy: *Anything else, Steve? You can talk about anything, you know.*
Me: *Okay. I need a gun to kill a bloody monster before it gets so big it breaks out of its cage and eats someone.*

Instead I'll sit there and listen as they tell me I could do one day a week bricklaying at the tech and do building site work the rest of the week. Don't get me wrong — I've got nothing against brickies. They make good money. But I don't want to be one. I've *never* had anyone ask if I wanted to take any GCSEs. Or do any A levels. I don't want to go to university, but imagine if I said I wanted to? They'd laugh me out of the room.

"Fun," repeats Jimmy. "I'll try to arrange something for the weekend. Maybe we could go go-karting or do a round of golf?"

"No, thanks, Jimmy. I'm a bit old for family outings."

Why would I want to go go-karting when I've been nicking cars since I was eight years old?

A flatbed truck draws up outside, and Jimmy goes to investigate.

I'm relieved. All this talk of fun makes me feel angry. How can I skip around like a happy teenager when I'm about to be thrown out onto the street? Are these people mad?

I glance out the window. Jimmy is talking to the truck driver.

I read the writing on the side of the truck: ERIC WINSTANLEY — BLACKSMITH.

I've heard Jimmy and Verity talking about this. The man's come to put up a fence. Probably to keep out scum like me. There's a dog in the front seat, a brown-and-white spaniel.

I wonder how Malackie is doing. I only hope my dear father remembers to feed him. But at least it means I can collect him as soon as I'm ready. As soon as I work out some sort of plan.

I go outside for a smoke. The bloke talking to Jimmy is about thirty years old and scruffy-looking. He's got hair even shorter than mine and a nose ring. I feel sorry for him. Imagine being named Eric! His dog is sticking its head out the window so I walk around to the van to talk to it. It has these crazy cross-eyes and sniffs my hand.

"He won't bite," calls the bloke. "He hasn't got any teeth left. He eats stones."

"What's he called?" I ask.

"I just call him Dog," says the bloke. "So there's no confusion."

I'm not sure about that. But then again, I don't expect the dog minds.

"Hello, Dog," I say, scratching its ears.

When the blacksmith has gone, Jimmy comes up to me.

"I'm really sorry about your dog," he says. "I don't think it would have worked out."

"Yeah, right," I say.

NINE

Carol gets a scooter for her birthday, this really cool Vespa, very sharp. I bet you can guess what color it is. Correct: pink. On my sixteenth birthday, Jimmy and Verity gave me a game for my Xbox and clothes vouchers for the Gap. The Gap!

Carol goes all around the driveway on it, shouting and showing off. She won't let me or Robert have a go.

Before I leave for work I have a good look at it. I prod the white leather seat and fiddle with the mileometer.

Carol comes up to me. "Don't you dare nick it," she says. "I know you want to."

"Now there's an idea," I say.

She put her hands on her hips. "I'll kill you if you touch it again," she says.

Naturally this is a challenge I cannot resist, so I grab the throttle and pull it back. "*Vroom, vroom,*" I say. I know this is childish of me, but I can't help myself.

"Very funny," she says. "But I mean it. I know what a tea leaf

68

you are. I expect you've already called up your mates who you can flog it to."

I walk over the gravel to my car.

"Happy birthday, little sis," I say, just to annoy her.

"I'm not your bloody sister."

I drive off, swerving closer to her than I should. I enjoy the look of alarm in her face before I steer away.

Naomi, the supervisor, doesn't say anything about my being away yesterday. She gives me a new beard net and set of gloves and tells me to join the kebab line. I'm prepared today. I've got four T-shirts on under my sweater and I'm wearing my thickest socks. The radio seems even louder than before, even though there aren't as many people around. I scan the line for the nice-looking girl I saw on the first day. She's here, talking to another girl with a pasty-white face. My girl's wearing tight black jeans under her white coat. I decide that my mission for the day is to find out her name. I am busy squashing all the mince into the kebab boxes when Naomi orders me to come with her. We go through into another underground room. There's no radio here but the layout is pretty much the same as the first. Naomi gives me a crate of dead chickens and tells me to put each one on a tray, ready to send down the conveyor belt for washing and dressing.

You know when your mum buys a chicken from the supermarket and it's all pinky-yellow and sitting neatly as a pussycat with all its giblets gone and its legs tucked in nicely? Well, they don't get like that on their own. Some mug like me has to wear a stupid hat and push them into shape. The chicken has to be plucked, gutted, and set. Not all chickens come through this process very well. They don't look very tasty. A wing might have been torn off, or the skin is ripped down one side. Some of the chickens are in a pretty bad way. Naomi shows me how to hide the obvious imperfections, while others she tells me to put aside so the meat can be stripped and turned into kebabs. The really manky ones she tells me to throw away.

You can imagine how I feel about throwing away meat. I keep thinking of my hungry Beast. I'll work something out, don't worry. It's funny how different the chickens are. In the supermarket they all look the same, don't they? But here some are flabby, some are scrawny. They vary in color from bright yellow to a nasty purple. By the time they leave the factory they'll look all sterile and uniform and the sort of thing that's easy to put in your shopping cart and forget was ever alive.

At lunchtime I engineer it so I'm sitting at the same table as the foxy girl. I ask her for a light, which she doesn't have, and I get a good look at her face. It is broader than I thought, which is quite a shock. The eyes are far apart, which gives her this calm sort of look. She has a small nose and a nice mouth. I give her an eight out of ten, but I can't really judge because she is wearing far too many clothes.

Her pasty mate gives me a light, and I sit smoking throughout my chips, giving the girl sneaky looks. I hear pasty-face call her Josie. I wonder if this is a nickname or if it's short for something.

"Crap, innit?" I say to her. Stephen, the master chat-up artist.

"Yeh." She gives me a nod and dives into her food. That, by

the way, is not a good sign. Selby says if a woman stuffs her face in front of you, then she is definitely not interested. Don't ask me why. I wonder if it's the same rule for men. Should I be piling into my chips? I decide not to worry about it. I'm too hungry to start pissing around.

It turns out it's the easiest thing ever to bag me a couple of moldy chickens. At the end of the day, like before, most people have gone. I am the only one in the chicken room except a couple of students who couldn't care less what I'm up to. I grab a new trash bag and stuff two chickens in, then sling it over my shoulder. If anyone asks, I'll say I'm taking them to the incinerator. But nobody says anything.

I chuck the bag in the trunk of my car. I realize that I can do this every day if I'm sneaky. The Beast will grow even bigger at this rate.

My car won't start. When I turn the ignition, there's nothing. Then I realize I left the lights on. It was foggy this morning.

"Shit." I smack the dashboard. What can I do? For a minute I'm tempted to nick someone else's car. There's a Vauxhall Cavalier parked next to me. It would be so easy. But I remember that I have enough to worry about without getting done for car theft. And I might get my license taken away. I can't risk it. Besides, I can't exactly drive it up the Reynoldses' drive, can I? What will I say? "My mate gave it to me"?

I'm fiddling around with the hood, just wasting time, really, before giving Jimmy a call, when I hear a truck pull over behind me.

It's the blacksmith bloke with the piercings.

He leans out the window.

"I thought I recognized you," he says.

71

"Do you work here?" I ask stupidly.

"No, I'm doing a job, welding up some crates. What's wrong with the motor?"

"Flat battery," I say.

Eric gets out of his truck. "I got some jump leads," he says. "Let's give them a go."

Eric chats quite a lot as we wait for my battery to charge. He invites me to sit in his truck with Dog. It's a real mess; bills, receipts, newspapers, chocolate wrappers, tools, and bits of metal lie everywhere.

"It needs a woman's touch," says Eric. "I'm too busy to tidy it out." He fishes a bag of nuts out of the dash. "Want some?" I nod, and he empties a handful into my palm before funneling the rest into his mouth.

"What's it like working here?" he asks after he's finished chewing and swallowing. Dog puts a dirty paw on my knee.

"Crap," I say.

There's a massive hammer wedged in between the seats. I pull it out and examine it. It could smash a skull with one blow.

"You interested in metalworking?" asks Eric.

"Dunno," I say, putting the hammer down.

Eric tells me about his business, and how he's about to expand into new premises, and how most of his work these days is curtain rods for posh people's living rooms, but what he really likes doing is construction work. He tells me he's just had a massive row with his girlfriend, but he's hoping they'll make up. I decide he's a bit soft but I quite like him. He has a pretty good

CD player but his music collection is terrible. It's all death metal and heavy rock.

"Do you nail shoes on horses?" I ask him.

"That's what a farrier does. I'm into metalworking."

When the battery has charged up a bit, Eric gives me a push and we bump start my car. I don't want to stop once I'm going so I shout "Cheers" out the window.

Eric nods. "Come around the workshop sometime," he says. "You might find it interesting."

I keep up the revs so I don't stall. My wheels spin over the tarmac.

The Reynoldses' house has this mad buzz about it. Verity is testing fairy lights, Jimmy is writing his name on all his CDs — as if anyone would want them! And I know Carol is somewhere close because I can smell her. She leaves these body sprays in the bathroom. They have crazy names like Mountain Fire and Purple Dream. Each one smells worse than the next.

I make myself a melted cheese sandwich and settle down to watch.

"What's going on?" I ask Verity as she switches on her lights.

She looks shifty. "Have you forgotten?" she says. "It's Carol's birthday party tonight."

Party! No one told me about it.

"Jimmy and I are going to the pub quiz," she says. "Robert's refusing to come with us."

I bet he is. Carol's got lots of tasty friends.

I find Robert in the downstairs bog, trying to pierce his ear. Blood is splattered all over the washbasin.

"The needle won't go through," he mutters. He looks a bit green.

"You need ice to numb the pain," I say.

Robert looks at me gratefully. "Get me some, will you, Stephen?"

I am dropping ice cubes into a mug in the kitchen when Carol appears. One of her eyelids is silver, the other is metallic green. I hate to admit it, but she looks great.

"I hope you're going out," she whispers to me.

"I knew nothing about it," I say honestly.

Carol leans closer. She has got shimmery skin. One of her presents was talcum powder with sparkles in it.

"They didn't tell you so you wouldn't invite any of your scummy mates," she says. "Not that you've got any."

I take a deep breath. "Well, I'm sorry to disappoint you," I say, "but I shall be here all evening."

Maybe I should feed her cat, Dudley, to the Beast. As a birthday present.

TEN

The front door closes. Robert, Carol, and I exchange glances.

"Right," says Carol. "Stephen, go and get me some cider and some cigarettes, will you? I'll pay you back later."

"Your parents will kill me if they know I've been buying you booze," I say. "Anyway, I'm underage, too."

"Just do it," she says. "They only left me a crate of lager shandy. I ask you, what was the point of that?"

I decide to do as she asks. What does it matter what Jimmy and Verity think of me? I'll be out of here soon enough. I know an offy in town where I can get served. I'm beginning to look forward to this party.

"Get a move on," says Carol. "People will start arriving in an hour."

When I get back I realize straightaway that something is not right. The house is quiet. I expect to see people beginning to arrive, but there's nobody here. I walk into the kitchen and notice the fairy lights are still on the counter.

"Hello?"

I search the house but don't find anyone. I sit at the bottom of the stairs and sigh.

After a short time I think I've realized what's going on. Before I leave the house I find Carol's schoolbag, which is wedged between the sofa cushions in the sitting room, and I remove her English and geography notebooks. She has just done her mock exams and is very pleased with herself because she got As. Very neatly, I tear six random pages from the geography notebook. These are covered in tables and charts and Carol's swirly blue handwriting. I fold the pages neatly, ease them into an empty Kettle Chips packet, and bury them in the bin. Robert never locks his room so I place the English book in a plastic bag under some smelly T-shirts in the bottom of his wardrobe. I'm too old for this sort of thing, but sometimes I just can't help it. I feel a tiny bit bad for Robert. He will suffer if and when the book is discovered, but he has played a role in this and deserves payback. All of this is sad, I know, but it makes me feel better. Now I can go along to the party. I'm fairly sure where it is, and I can be calm. I think Carol and Robert have gotten off lightly.

The village hall is half a mile up the road. As I expect, there are crowds of teenagers hanging around outside. Music is blaring out from the doors. People are being dropped off. I park and saunter inside.

Carol is swigging from a bottle of whiskey.

"Stephen," she shouts over the music, "where are my cigarettes?" I hand them over with the cider. She is with a couple of her mates. One of them is okay, but the other is a right minger. They're all wearing shedloads of makeup. "You found us, then?" says Carol, sniggering. She's only talking to me because she's with her mates. They are all looking at me so I walk off. I find

Robert annoying the DJ. I am pleased to say he at least looks guilty when he sees me.

"She said she'd kick me in the knackers if I told you where the party really was," he says. I believe him and give him a can of Stella.

"Make it last 'cos that's all you're having," I say. The hall's practically empty because everyone's outside. I don't blame them; it's really bright in here. Like a club when they turn all the lights on to get rid of everyone.

There's a tap on my arm.

"Candles," says Carol. "There's some in the kitchen drawer. Go and get them for me, will you, Stephen, *please*?"

I stare down at her. I never realized how small she is next to me.

"Why, are you planning to move the party somewhere else?" I ask.

She smiles nastily. "You might as well make yourself useful since you are technically a gate-crasher."

"No," I say.

To my surprise Carol does not insist.

"Robert," she says. "Candles, fetch." As if she's talking to a dog.

Her mates giggle and Robert looks uncomfortable.

"Robert," she says, "you know what will happen if you disobey me."

"Don't be tight," says the minger mate. I decide she's not so bad after all.

"I'll tell everyone about your little secret," says Carol. "Your sex box."

"Shut up," says Robert. He looks really upset.

"Leave him alone," I say. "Go and get the candles yourself."

At this point, luckily for Robert, a bloke Carol fancies comes into the hall.

"Terry," she shrieks, and bounces over. "Have you gotten me a present?"

I turn to Robert. "Let's get some air," I say.

Outside there is some hard drinking going on. I reckon there's about fifty or sixty kids, and most of them are knocking back something or other. Some have already paired off, but mostly the blokes are on one side of the parking lot, and the girls are on the other. Robert and I go and sit on the cricket pitch and I roll a joint.

"Give us a puff on that," says Robert when it's made.

"You're too young," I say.

"This is a medicinal necessity," he says. "Please."

I hand it over. Robert puffs away like he has the lungs of an old Rasta.

"Go easy on that," I say. "I'm not letting you get addicted."

Robert hands it back and settles down on his elbows.

"What did I do in my former life to deserve such a sister?" he says.

"Robert," I ask, "what exactly is this sex box?" I've found it, of course, but Robert always keeps it locked.

Robert grins and taps the side of his nose.

"You're too innocent, bro," he says.

Later, I'm scanning the girls to see if there's anything I like the look of. I must need a girlfriend because none of them look too bad. Even the girl I thought was a minger has taken off her sweater and is wearing this tiny vest that shows off her tits and belly.

The party is beginning to take off. People are shouting and running and one boy is puking into an ice cream container. The DJ has turned up the music and people are dancing in the parking lot. A crowd of boys is doing a lot of coughing from inside the ladies' room. Carol has gotten hold of loads of candles and is lighting them all around the hall. She turns the lights out and everyone cheers. They look good but I have to move one when it starts to turn the wall behind it black.

"You need to watch these," I say. "The whole place could go up."

"Oh, piss off," says Carol.

Outside, Robert sits on a car hood surrounded by Carol's mates. They are calling him sweet and patting his hair.

"Look at the legs on that one," he whispers to me as I walk by. I turn to see who he is gawping at. She is wearing a short skirt that shows off her long, slim legs. My eyes travel up her body to her face. Even in the gloom I can see it's Josie, the girl from the meat factory.

I want to go and talk to her, but I'm too scared. What would I say? She's with all these other girls. She probably won't recognize me anyway. She catches me watching her and gives me a smile. I feel incredible, like I've just found a load of money or something. I find an unopened can of lager and take it over.

"Hello," I say. "Do you want a drink?"

She takes the can. "I thought I recognized you," she says. "Murray's, right?" She has quite a deep voice.

"Yep, kebab line," I say. There is an awkward pause. "I'm

Stephen." I feel like a right knob, but she smiles and tells me what I already know, that her name is Josie.

We carry on like this, slagging off the meat factory and its occupants. She is quite easy to talk to and her mates seemed to have fallen away from us. I look down and see I've crushed my beer can into a little disc. I drop it and hope Josie hasn't noticed.

There's a load of shouting from inside the hall and I hear the showers being switched on. I look around for Robert, but he is still sitting on the car hood surrounded by his ladies. He looks like he's having the time of his life. He makes me laugh, that kid.

Splashing noises and yelling comes from the showers. A boy comes running out into the parking lot. He is soaked, pissed, and very pleased with himself. He goes up to these girls and shakes himself like a dog. They all scream.

"Do you want some?" Josie offers me a swig from the can.

"No, thanks," I say, watching the wet kid pushing down the hood of the car, trying to set off the alarm. He pushes so hard, Robert slips off. I decide not to get pissed. Someone has to keep an eye on Robert. I've seen parties like these turn nasty. He's still too young, really. Verity and Jimmy should have made him go with them.

In the corner of the parking lot there are a couple of lads sniffing lighter fluid. I watch and feel worried. What's happening to me? I've done it myself. But you've got to be careful. I know this kid who died doing it. But I can hardly go over there and tell them, can I?

"Great party," says Josie. I wonder if she's being serious. I also wonder if she has a boyfriend. I am about to ask her outright when there is all this screaming from the showers.

"Where my closes?"

A couple of lads push past me and dump something in a Dumpster. Next thing is they've grabbed the lighter fluid off the others and are pouring it in. A kid lights a match and drops it in and *WHOOSH*, the Dumpster is full of flames.

A naked boy comes running out and everyone laughs. The boy can hardly stand he is so drunk, and he is trying to cover up his prick with his beer can.

"Wha've done with my close?" he burbles.

Somebody wolf whistles.

"Look at his white bum," shrieks a girl.

I look around for Carol. This party is getting seriously out of hand.

Naked boy collapses and lies facedown on the concrete.

"Someone should cover him up," says Josie.

I agree but I'm reluctant to part with my jacket. We watch as his so-called mates take turns giving him little kicks.

Then this crazy thing rushes out of the hall. It's Carol.

"What have you done to him, you bastards?" she shrieks.

The kid on the ground is in a bad way. He's passed out, and brown fluid is dribbling out of his mouth. Someone ought to roll him over so he doesn't choke on his vomit.

Nobody does.

"Wake up, Terry," says Carol. She shakes his shoulder. Terry! It's the bloke she fancies.

I sidle up to her.

"Don't think much of your taste in men," I say. Reluctantly I take his arm and roll him on his side, trying not to look at his dick flopping around. Then I take off my jacket. It will probably get covered in sick and I haven't got another one. I cover him up.

81

Somebody shines a flashlight on him. Brown stuff is still running out of his mouth and I see the whites of his eyes as his eyeballs roll up into his head.

"Terry, it's me, Carol." She kneels by his side.

"Your woman needs you, Tezza," says some bloke, and they all laugh.

Terry starts choking and they laugh some more. The smell of the burning clothes is stinking out the parking lot. Some girls start coughing. Then the DJ puts on this kick-ass tune and really cranks up the volume and everyone starts going in the hall.

I am just going off to find Josie when Carol grabs my sleeve.

"What am I going to do?" she asks. I try to pull away but she won't let go. "Stephen, you've got to help," she says.

"He'll be all right, he's just pissed." I shake her off and squint through the crowd. I can't see Josie anywhere. Then I spot her. Some huge kid is chatting her up, leaning against the wall with her behind him. Who the hell is he?

"I don't think . . ." mumbles Carol.

"Oh, chill out," I say. "At least this way you might get your wicked way with him."

I can see Josie's shadowy face and she is laughing at something the big bloke has said. I didn't make her laugh. I wonder if he'll punch me if I go over. I decide he's not her boyfriend. If he was, they'd be snogging or else he'd be ignoring her. No, this is a chat-up scene I'm watching, and I'm not going to stand around and let it happen. I blow in my hands to check my breath and saunter over.

Carol's voice cuts through the night and the music.

"He's not breathing."

Everything seems to go quiet.

ELEVEN

Of course it's muggins here who ends up taking Carol's man to the emergency room. As soon as he starts puking his guts up and she realizes he's just wasted, she refuses to come with me. She doesn't want anything to do with the situation in case it gets worse. But I don't reckon it will. He's just drunk. I've seen it a million times. She should be worrying about the kids doing the lighter fuel. That's dangerous.

"I can't leave my own party," she says. "I need to keep an eye on things."

I know what she means. It's pretty wild. But if I was Terry I'd be pretty pissed that she won't come. What kind of a girlfriend is that? Not that Carol is his girlfriend.

I reckon the real reason Carol won't come is because she's scared, simple as that.

Part of the reason I let her off is I think someone should watch out for Robert. I want to take him with me but he refuses. I don't blame him. He's found himself a bottle of red wine and is sharing it with three gorgeous sixteen-year-olds. As for me, I don't even get to say a proper good-bye to Josie.

Bloody Carol.

Have you ever been to the emergency room on a Friday night? It's not a pretty sight. There are loads of drunks, like Terry, and blokes running around with blood streaming down their faces, as well as normal people who have broken an arm or are having an asthma attack.

The nurse on duty gives me this filthy look as I drag Terry in over the shiny floor. He's sobering up a bit now and is coming out with all this crap about his exams. I dump him in a chair and a nurse comes and I answer the questions as best as I can.

Full name?	Don't know
How much has he drunk?	Don't know
How old?	Don't know
Address?	Don't know
Parents' phone number?	Don't know

I've wrapped the car seat cover round his middle and he's still wearing my jacket so at least he isn't flashing anymore. He slumps in the chair and the nurse calls for assistance.

At this point I leave him to it. Don't blame me. He's in safe hands and I'm not going to sit around all night in that scummy place with doctors giving me dirty looks like it's all my fault. Besides, I'm worried about Robert. You know when you get that kind of feeling that something is going to go badly wrong? Well, I've got that feeling now. Like something bad is going to happen at the party and I want to get back there.

Look at me! Mr. Worry. I must be getting old. By rights I should be piling in the drink with the rest of them, trying to score with anything in a skirt. Maybe that's the real reason I'm so keen to get back. I definitely want to catch Josie. I don't want her thinking I'm not interested, especially since I've got competition.

I drive up the hill, back to the village hall. I'm just passing the Reynoldses' house when I catch up with a fire engine. Don't ask how fast I was going — you'd be putting your foot down too if you had a bird like Josie on the cards. It's typical of Carol to mess things up for me. If I hadn't taken Terry to hospital, I might be getting off with Josie on the cricket pitch right now. I watch the blue lights flashing. I wonder how far she'd let me go.

To my surprise the fire engine is slowing. There is an orange glow in the sky. I pull over. Three other fire engines are in the parking lot of the village hall. The flames are so high and so bright the whole night is lit up. I can see that a whole part of the roof has collapsed and smoke is pouring out. All these firefighters are pointing their hoses. I turn off my engine and get out. I am hit by the smell of smoke, and there's lots of shouting.

Someone is talking through a megaphone.

"EVERYONE STAY AT THE FAR END OF THE CRICKET PITCH. MAKE NO ATTEMPT TO ENTER THE HALL. I REPEAT, STAY AT THE FAR END OF THE CRICKET PITCH. DO NOT ENTER THE HALL."

I stare at the flames. I've never seen a fire so big. Even when we set fire to the trash can in the school playground all those years ago. There is a mini explosion and all these golden sparks fill the sky. It's quite amazing, really. I find I'm enjoying myself. I'm absolutely not guilty of any of this. I can lean back and enjoy the show. I can't find my cigarettes so I have to roll a joint. The shadows of Carol's mates move at the far end of the field. I bet they've all sobered up now. I could climb through the hedge and run across the field to join them, but I'm quite happy where I am. Outside it all, just watching.

A car draws up behind me and a middle-aged woman gets out. She ignores me and runs into the parking lot. A fireman comes to meet her and turns her back.

"But I just want to know my son is safe," she says. Her voice ends in this kind of wail. Like an animal. She's walked back to her car and told to wait. I hope Josie's okay. But she was hanging around outside for most of the evening, and she wasn't pissed. I have the feeling she can look after herself. Then I remember Robert and get panicky. Did he have the sense to stay outside? Is he with all the dark figures at the end of the field? I don't trust Carol to make sure he's all right. I should have taken him with me. Why did I leave him here with all these maniacs?

I decide to get through the hedge and find Robert when I hear a car pull up behind me. I assume it's another parent and keep climbing.

"Hang on, son," says a male voice.

I twist my neck round and curse. It's the cops. I decide to pretend I haven't heard him. I don't want to draw attention to myself. In the dark he wouldn't recognize me. But I haven't gone very far before I feel a hand on my collar.

I am pulled unceremoniously down the bank and onto the road.

"I said wait," the copper snaps. He shines a flashlight in my face and then at the rolly in my hand. "And what the hell have you been up to?"

Some people reckon they are born under a lucky star, or that a guardian angel is looking out for them. That's not me. This girl once said to me that you make your own fate and luck has nothing to do with it. All I can say is I hope I do better in the future.

Everything you do leaves scars. Like when I got bitten by my affectionate little pet. I reckon all those cars I nicked, all the stuff I robbed, the vandalism, the broken bottles, the glue, everything, it all still shows, though I've been pretty clean for over a year. And that's why the cop nicks me. Every bad thing I've done before shows in my face.

The copper cuffs me and bundles me into the back of his police car. He's got me Breathalyzed (thankfully the beer I had earlier has worn off), takes away my watch and car keys, and bangs me up in a cell within the hour. He's found my file on the computer and seen that I've been in trouble for arson before. As far as he's concerned I am guilty as charged.

I sit on the thin plastic mattress. I count the bricks in the gray wall. There is a stain on the floor that looks like a bear. I shiver in this jumpsuit thing. They've taken my clothes away to test them. You see, the copper reckons I set fire to the village hall. But you know I didn't do it, don't you? You know I'd taken that dozy kid to the emergency room? I know I just have to keep my cool and the truth will come out. Loads of people saw me drive Terry off.

A man is led past my cell and he is shouting and swearing. He sounds pissed. I hope they don't put him in here with me. A beating is the last thing I need. There's the clink of keys and the sound of a lock turning and the creak of a door. Then the shouting gets muffled. Thank God for that. The piss head is next door.

I reckon Jimmy will come and get me out soon. What had they said? That there would probably be a lock-in at the Globe and they'd be back at one o'clock in the morning? He'd get the truth out of Carol and Robert.

Carol.

I swear out loud. There's no way she's going to tell the truth. Of course they're going to blame me. She's not going to own up to the candles. I knew they were dodgy. She's not going to tell Mummy and Daddy that her little friends were sniffing lighter fluid in the parking lot. She's not going to admit her beloved was so wasted he was practically pissing himself. Why would she start telling the truth now? My only hope is Robert.

The hours go by. I lie on the bed and watch the walls grow lighter, my stomach aching.

At seven o'clock in the morning the guard brings me a cup of tea. I'm so thirsty I burn the skin off my tongue. The tea is cheap and nasty and smells cheesy. The milk must be off. I need to blow my nose but there is only this tracing paper bog roll, so I use the sleeve of the jumpsuit. I feel like shit. I'm going to end up like my dad whether I like it or not. No wonder he chooses to live outside after being shut up in a tiny room like this for so long. I want to get out of here so much it hurts. I wipe my nose again. I wipe it so much it gets sore and my sleeve is damp. I must be allergic to something. The mattress is probably rammed full of fleas and bugs. Horrible little aliens you can only see under a microscope.

Where the hell is Jimmy?

My stomach hurts worse every minute.

At ten-twenty someone finally unlocks my door. I expect to see the guard and to be led up to the interview room. I expect Jimmy to be there.

The door swings open.

It's Mindy.

TWELVE

Mindy's wearing a long purple hippie skirt, with a black T-shirt so tight I can see the rolls of fat round her waist. Her hair is screwed up into a bun and she has pink lipstick smeared on her mouth. She carries a large green file.

"Oh, Steve," says Mindy. "You've been doing so well up to now."

I look away. Is this what they teach these people at Social Worker School?

"The Reynoldses think you were jealous because you hadn't been invited to the party," says Mindy. "Correct?"

Has she never heard of "innocent until proven guilty"? Man, have I ever got the wrong social worker. This woman hates me. I don't know why. Maybe she is scared of me. I am bigger than she is. And maybe it has penetrated even her thick skull that I don't give a toss about her. These people need to be liked. I know that. Why else would they do such a shitty job?

"Apparently you were very angry last night," says Mindy. She puts a veiny hand on my shoulder. She's wearing old-woman rings. "I expect you felt rejected and I believe you're upset about St. Mark's."

"I didn't set fire to the hall."

I don't know why I bother saying it. It won't make any difference. Mindy has imagined the whole thing already. Evil Stephen with his can of petrol. His jealous rage. The lit match.

Mindy gives a little sigh, which she probably thinks is cute and humorous. Then she looks around to check where she's put her handbag.

"You're going to have to stay here a while, I'm afraid. Then they are going to transfer you to the young offenders' institute at Bailbridge."

I nearly laugh then. I'll be meeting up with lots of familiar faces.

Sometimes it seems that my future has been all mapped out, and nothing I do will make any difference.

"I took Carol's boyfriend, Terry, to the emergency room last night," I say. "I couldn't have done it. The place was a firetrap anyway. There were all these candles, and Carol . . ."

Mindy interrupts.

"I'll arrange for your things to be collected from the Reynoldses'," she says. "I don't expect they'll want you back after this. Do you?"

I tell her to eff off.

Do you blame me?

Mindy gathers her file, shaking her head. "We are all disappointed in you, Stephen. But most of all you've let yourself down."

I turn away. I shouldn't let that woman get to me. I should've learned by now to ignore anything she says.

I stare at the wall.

* * *

At 11:45 I have a lunch of mushy peas and ham and straight after I am taken upstairs to an interview room. A policeman tells me they have found four empty bottles of lighter fluid. Someone has checked out the hospital and there is video evidence of my presence there. Several kids have backed up my story already.

I'd like an apology but I don't get it.

I am taken home in a police car. And when I get there I find Carol crying on the sofa. I imagine it's because she is in trouble about the fire.

"Hey, Carol," I say cheerfully. "How about this? Two arsonists in one house!"

"Robert's in the hospital," she says.

Her eyes are puffy and she's wearing her old yellow dressing gown. She looks about twelve years old.

"He inhaled too much smoke and passed out," she says. "They took him away in an ambulance." Her nose is running and she doesn't bother to wipe it.

I collapse in the armchair opposite. Why did I take that useless kid to the ER? I knew something was going to go wrong. I could have foreseen all of this. I could have prevented it.

I can't do anything but sit and stare.

We hear the crunch of tires on gravel.

"Please don't mention the candles," says Carol. "They think the fire spread from the Dumpster."

"It won't make any difference," I say. "They'll find out that candles started it. There'll be forensic evidence."

"Please, Stephen." Carol sits up and wipes her face. Suddenly she looks sixteen again.

I have a flashback to all the times Carol lied to get me into trouble. Right from the first day I didn't stand a chance with this family. They always took her side, even if they said they believed me.

I shrug. "Makes no odds to me," I say. "How's Terry?"

She colors up.

"He's okay," she says slowly. She feels her neck. "Thanks," she says. The word nearly chokes her, I can tell.

Jimmy comes in alone. He's left Verity at the hospital. He looks at the ceiling and says that Robert is going to be all right, but that they have to keep him in for a few days.

The relief is incredible.

"Can I go and see him?" I ask.

Jimmy finally looks at me.

"No, Stephen. He needs to be kept quiet."

He blames me for the fire. I can see it in his face. Despite the evidence, he still thinks it was me. I feel this wave of anger. I haven't had such a good night myself. I've been in the slammer, and no one came to get me out. But then Jimmy takes a step towards me and pats my arm.

"You all right?" he asks.

I shrug. No thanks to him.

Carol starts to say something nasty and changes her mind. I never saw her do that before. Things have changed between us. I can feel it. I've got her on a string now.

The thing is I just don't care enough to take advantage of it.

* * *

I'm sitting on the garden swing at the Reynoldses', tickling Dog behind his ears and watching Eric the blacksmith measure the wall.

"Math," he says. "It's all math."

He asks me to hold the tape and I end up writing all the figures in his notebook for him.

"How's the boy?" he asks, nodding at the house.

"Better," I say. "He came out of the hospital yesterday."

Robert is a little paler than usual but full of mad stories about how he hallucinated from the smoke and about the sexy nurses giving him bed baths. He has to keep quiet for a bit but he's all right.

"I heard you took Terry Dunleary to the hospital. That true?" Eric takes the notebook from me.

"Yeah," I say, surprised.

"Well, thanks," says Eric.

I must have given him a funny look.

"He's my sister's boy," he explains. "He's always getting into trouble. He's a plonker, that kid."

I nod. "Not everyone thinks so," I say.

Eric finishes measuring and whistles for Dog.

"You still at the meat factory?" he asks.

"Kind of," I say.

I'm planning to leave and get something better, but I don't know what. I know I should stay there for now. I'm going to have to show my face there tomorrow or they'll sack me. But I really don't want to go back. It's not that the people are so bad, and if I work quick enough I can get warm. But I hate the sight of all that meat and mess, and I hate the smell. It makes me feel ill. And all that death makes me feel queasy. It's a sick place, really. A massive building dedicated to cutting up animals. It's like a horror film. (Listen to me! I sound like a girl! I'm going soft.)

"Listen," says Eric. "Jimmy has suggested you come and help me in the workshop some mornings. He said you weren't particularly happy at the meat factory."

Fancy Jimmy sussing that.

I eye Eric suspiciously. "I suppose he's paying you?"

"He said Social Services would give me something," Eric admits. "What do you think?"

I don't know. I've never thought about it. I have a brief fantasy about me standing by a massive furnace, heating up red-hot metal and walloping it into a sword.

"Why not?" I say.

Eric's workshop is this big shed with unpainted breeze block walls and an uneven concrete floor. He's got a large metal table, which he calls his welding bench, and there are bits of metal and machinery lying everywhere. He gives me this safety talk when I arrive. Don't touch any tools or machinery or metal unless he says so. The metal might be hot and some of the machinery could take my fingers off. I like the forge best. It's like a massive open fire with a hood. It's all piled up with coal and there's a fan underneath to keep it hot. I stand close to it, warming my hands.

"That's a cast-iron stand, made in the last century," says Eric. He shoves some wood in to stop it from going out. There's a silver metal flue that goes right out through the roof. Eric's got the windows and double doors wide open because, he says, it's important to keep the place well ventilated. But I like the smell. It's a clean, burning smell, a bit like wood smoke.

Eric goes on about the difference between cast iron and wrought iron, and I drift off a bit. I can't keep up with him but am too embarrassed to ask him to explain it again. Eric tells me that he makes many of his tools as he needs them. How cool is that? But then he goes into detail about the differences between his hammers, and my concentration wanders off again.

Some of the machines look really evil. I hope he lets me use them. Eric is wearing a leather apron and steel-toe-cap boots. My sneakers are no good for this place. The dust has made them shitty already.

He shows me this machine called a Linisher. It's like a sanding belt for metal. Eric gets this iron bar and switches on the machine and holds the bar next to the belt. The sparks go flying. Eric switches the machine off and shows me the bar. It's got a perfect curve on it.

"I might get you to do some of that at some point," he says.

But Eric doesn't let me use any of the machines. Instead he makes me sweep up, make the tea, and carry in sacks of coal. After that he asks me to tidy the yard outside. I ask him how he wants it and he says it's up to me. So I spend about two hours stacking steel rods and collecting rubbish and moving disused machinery. It's grunt work but I don't mind. The yard looks miles better than it did. When I'm finished, Eric is dead chuffed because now he can fit his truck into the yard.

Eric says I can come in whenever I like if I give him a ring. And I think I might, though since I'm not getting paid, I have to stick with the meat factory. But I reckon if I came here long enough, I could be a proper blacksmith like Eric. Maybe one day I'd have my own forge and my own truck. It's all right working here. It takes my mind off things. I decide I'll come in a couple of mornings a week. If I was at the meat factory every day I'd go mad. And I don't think they'll sack me. I'm a good worker. I don't piss around like most of the lads. I don't gob in the kebabs or mess around much. And like I said, they are pretty relaxed about when people turn up. You just get your time sheet signed and that's it.

If Eric teaches me to weld, I might be able mend the water cage.

THIRTEEN

Me and Robert are playing chess on his bed and he's hammering me. (See, I might not have gone to school much, but at least I know how to play chess.) Robert's killed all my pieces except my king, which he is harassing around the board. I hear footsteps on the gravel outside. I'm surprised, as it's late, nearly ten o'clock. But the doorbell goes off, playing this lamby tune. Soon enough, Jimmy is calling me.

"Stephen, your dad's come to see you."

My dad! I look at Robert and he looks at me. He throws back his duvet and jumps out of bed.

"Where are you going?" I ask.

"I want a look," he says, running to the door.

I scratch my head. My dad has never come to visit me before. None of my family has, except Chas, and that's only twice-yearly visits carefully organized by Mindy. So what's my old man doing here?

Carol's lurking on the landing, trying to listen to the talk downstairs. There it is — his horrible growly voice. It sounds like he puts it on, but he doesn't. It's always been like that and it's worse indoors. I listen with Carol for a few minutes but I can't make out anything.

"Don't you want to see him?" she asks. I don't know if she is taking the piss or not.

"Stephen," Jimmy calls again.

I walk down the stairs. I have no idea what to expect. Come to think of it, how the hell did he find out my address?

Jimmy looks worried. I don't blame him. I wouldn't want this crazy-looking tramp in my house either. There are patches of mud on the carpet where he's walked. I thought he smelled pretty bad when I saw him in the forest but now he stinks worse than fresh sick. I ought to open a window. He hasn't made any effort to clean himself up or anything. He's wearing this dirty red jacket and old man's trousers that are too big. He's got bits in his beard. Dudley wakes up, takes one look at him, and legs it, shooting through my legs and up the stairs. My dad sits in Jimmy's armchair and I try not to look at the stains on his trousers.

"Where's Malackie?" I ask. I should have never given him to my dad to look after. He's probably dead by now. My dad can't even look after himself.

My dad makes a wet noise with his mouth.

"He's all right."

Jimmy hovers. He looks at the clock and notices Robert peeping round the door.

"Bed," he orders, and Robert vanishes.

Verity bustles in with a mug of tea and hands it to my dad so that the handle is pointing his way so he won't burn his fingers. He doesn't deserve this sort of treatment.

It's my fault he is here, stinking up the living room and

dribbling tea into his beard. If I was the Reynoldses, I'd throw the mug away as soon as he was gone.

There's a suppressed cough from the stairs. I feel sorry for Carol too — having random tramps in your house can't be very nice. Then I remember: Soon I'll be out of here and they won't have to put up with this sort of thing. Not until they get the next kid anyway.

"It's quite late," says Jimmy. "Would you like to come back and see Stephen in the morning? He has to be up early. He's got himself a job."

"Got nowhere to stay," says my dad.

I cringe as Verity and Jimmy exchange glances. *Please don't ask him to stay*. I stare at Jimmy and shake my head so slightly he probably doesn't notice.

But Jimmy isn't falling for it.

"We'll leave you two to talk," he says. "And after that, I'll be happy to give you a lift."

They leave us alone.

"What are you feeding him?" I ask.

My dad looks confused.

"The dog?" I remind him.

He waves his hand dismissively. "I told you, he's fine." He looks crafty. "Anything decent to drink round here?"

"No," I say.

"Got yourself a nice little pad here," says my dad, looking at the TV and DVD player, the stereo and speakers.

"Not for much longer." I stand behind the sofa because I don't want to sit down. "I told you before — they're kicking me out in a fortnight."

"Ah," says my dad.

It wouldn't surprise me at all if, in a month or so, the Reynolds family gets burgled.

I watch him check out the velvet curtains, the red carpet, the painting of the tree on the wall, the wood stove, the pile of *Good Housekeeping* magazines. He fingers the leather strap of one of Carol's discarded shoes and eyes a half-eaten Mars bar on the coffee table. I study his dreadlock. It's attached to the back of his head by two or three thin locks of hair. A couple of snips with the scissors and the whole thing would come off.

My dad swigs the last of his tea. "I want to see it," he says. "Show me where it is."

I gesture for him to keep his voice down because Carol is probably listening to every word.

"Why?" I whisper. "Are you going to help?"

The mug rolls off the chair to the floor.

"I'm interested," he says, "to find out if you are as big a liar as your mother."

I look at him for a long time. I want to punch him but I need his help.

"Will you help me get rid of it?" I ask finally.

"I'll phone the zoo for you. Just show me where the bloody thing is." He looks exasperated, and a thought strikes me.

"Have you been looking for it?"

"All bloody day," says my dad. "I reckon you've been lying to me, Stephen."

I want to spit in his face. Instead I retrieve the mug from the carpet and place it on the table.

Have you ever been playing a game, like chess or something, where you get so bored, you just want it to be over? When you start doing stupid things, like going on a killing spree and putting your queen in danger, just for some excitement or so you can be out? I love that feeling of losing. When everyone else is crowded around, getting wound up over a board and a few bits of plastic, you can just walk off and get some food. Or go outside and have a cigarette and feel the wind on your face. I get so restless sometimes, I'll do anything to escape. I feel like this now.

"I might be able to help," says my dad.

I don't think there's anything he can do apart from getting me a gun. But I'm fed up with being the only one who knows about this thing. When he sees it, he might realize what a problem I've got.

"All right," I say. "I'll take you up there."

He leaves a smell behind him. I look at the dent in the chair where he's been sitting. There is a leaf and crumbs of dirt on the seat. I wipe them off.

"He didn't want a lift, then?" says Jimmy, coming back into the room. "Where is he staying?"

"In the shed," I answer, grinning at Jimmy. "Only joking."

Jimmy, however, goes to the window and peers out. There is a full yellowy moon sitting on the treetops.

"Did he really say that?" he asks with a worried voice.

"Nah," I said. "Though I wouldn't put it past him."

Jimmy pulls the curtains and leaves the room. I hear him lock the front door, then go around to the back.

"Watch out, he might come down the chimney," I mutter.

"What was that?" Verity bustles in. She looks flustered. I

don't blame her. Like I said, my dad is not someone you'd want lounging round your house.

"Did he want anything in particular?" she fishes.

I have to tell her something convincing.

"He wants to borrow some money," I reply.

This seems to go down all right. Verity nods. "Did you give him any?"

I shake my head. "I need every penny at the moment, don't I?"

I am pleased to say she looks guilty.

"Stephen, I know you're upset at moving out. . . ."

I interrupt. "Not enough to set fire to the village hall, Verity."

I'm also pleased with this and decide it's my cue to go to bed.

Carol's door is closing just as I get to the top of the stairs. I wonder how much she has heard, how much she has worked out. Like I said, sometimes I do stupid things, just so I can get out of the game. Or to make it more interesting.

He's late, of course. I hang around the parking lot, feeling shifty as hell. I don't usually come in the public entrance because I'm likely to be carrying something big and dead to feed my boy. And I like to come at night. I feel exposed here, next to a notice and a trash can. But I couldn't rely on my dad to find the right spot, so I told him to meet me here. The warden drives past and I give him a wave because I haven't got time to hide. He waves back and drives on. I let out my breath.

Where is that scumbag? I wish I'd never agreed to this. What do I think I can get out of it? I half think I should just bugger off before he gets here. Dad never sorts things out. He only messes them up. But he does have contacts. He knows people who can help. As soon as he sees it, he'll want to help me. Anybody would.

I read on the Internet these animals haven't changed since prehistoric times and that they are millions of years old. My friend, I am dealing with a bloody dinosaur!

"Stephen."

It is the voice of my dear father.

He's leaning against the hood of a Range Rover. I never heard him coming. I notice he's carrying a big stick.

"Where did you sleep?" I ask.

"There." He points to the information shelter at the end of the lot. I see a pile of tins under the bench and an empty wrapper skiddling over the tarmac.

I feel self-conscious talking to him. I mean, he doesn't exactly blend in. An old couple in a sky-blue Rover pulls up next to us. The woman gives us a horrible look.

"Come on," I say.

With each step I feel more reluctant. It's unusual to see all these visitors. There's a much bigger reservoir not far away, with sailing and nature walks and all that sort of stuff. Most people go there. Now there are fishermen and walkers and even a couple of rowboats on the water. We have to be careful.

My dad goes over on his ankle.

"Bollocks."

He swears even more when he starts hobbling after me. We must look strange. There's me, seventeen years old, in my jeans and sneakers and hoodie, and this gross old tramp with the massive cod hanging from his head.

"How far?" moans my father. And, "Got anything to eat?"

I give him a banana. He peels it and chucks the skin into the water.

I check to see there is no one around. "Do you know anyone who can get me a gun?" I ask.

I've never looked properly into my dad's eyes before. They have these yellowy flecks, like sparks. I look away.

"Let me just see the thing," pants my dad.

He's in bad shape. He can hardly keep up with me, and his ankle doesn't help. But I'm not slowing down just so the old piss head doesn't get out of breath. I don't feel as wary of him as I normally do, maybe because he just looks like an old waster, like thousands of others. He's nothing near as sharp as he was last night in the Reynoldses' sitting room.

By the time we're getting near the water cage he is moaning and grumbling almost nonstop. He mutters under his breath. I try not to listen but I can't help hearing a few words. None of them are very complimentary about me.

I look up and down the path. I can't see anyone, but I don't feel right. I tell myself it's because I have my father with me. No one has ever been here with me before.

"Shhh," I tell my dad. It feels strange ordering him around. I half expect him to belt me. But instead he quiets down.

We step from the path and I lead him through the trees.

This is a big mistake. I know it. Maybe it's not too late. I could tell him right now that I've been winding him up. We could stop and go back. I could drop him back at his shed in the wood. Maybe if I wasn't being kicked out of the Reynoldses'

105

I would have done just that. Maybe if I was sure the cage was safe.

Dad moans like hell when we get to the thorn hedge.

"I'm not going through that, Stephen."

I ignore him and push through. If he's come this far, he won't stop now. After a short while I hear grumbling and snapping noises behind me.

From a distance the cage looks harmless enough. There are brambles growing up one side and at the back. You can't tell how big it is until you get right up close.

My dad kicks the bars.

"What have you got in there, Stephen?" he asks. There is the sound of water swirling round. He stops kicking and stares at me.

I peer through the bars. There is a horrible smell, like something rotting. I've never noticed it before. As my eyes get used to the gloom I see a gray wing stuck to one of the bars. Poor old pigeon. I look at the dark swirl of water. There's a new line of green algae growing up the walls and something is floating at the back of the cage, bobbing on the water. It's a small hoofed foot with wisps of yellowy wool stuck to it. I lean back in disgust. There are lots of lambs grazing around the reservoir. How the hell had one gotten in here? It must have gotten through the bars somehow and fallen in. I shudder. I play the scenario in my head — the bleating lamb kicking in the water and the sudden surfacing of the head and snout. His lunge. It makes me feel sick. But then I remember. The more he has to eat, the less likely it is that he will escape.

"I can't see anything," says my dad. "You're having me on."

I suddenly feel very tired.

"You'll see him if you get on top of the bars and look down."

I sound detached. My voice isn't my own; it's like I'm speaking underwater. I pass my father the key. "Crawl over till you reach the hatch," I say. "Then take a look inside. You can see him better from above, but you might have to lean over." I can hardly believe that at last someone else is going to see him and realize just how dangerous he is.

My father grabs one of the bars and gives it a yank.

"Is this thing going to take my weight?" he asks.

"It's metal but some of the bars are loose." I hand him a dead chicken out of my rucksack. "If you drop this in, he'll come right up to the surface."

My father gives me a funny look, as if he's trying to work out what I am thinking.

But I'm not thinking anything anymore. My mind is blank.

I watch as he clambers up the cage and balances himself on the bars at the top.

He is quite old now, my dad. He hasn't got very good balance. Years of drinking have seen to that. And he's not very clever. He thinks he is going to feed his son's pet, like giving a dog a bone, like feeding seed to a budgie. Part of me feels sad. Me and my boy have made it alone for years. Now it's all over.

"Where's Malackie?" I ask.

"With a mate," says my dad.

I watch as he shuffles over the bars. His arms wave around as he tries to keep steady. The metal creaks beneath him and I think I can hear some kind of noise coming from the water. But it's like white noise, like the TV isn't tuned in properly. I can't get a grip on the exact location.

My father has reached the hatch. He turns the key in the padlock and opens the lid. He lets it fall back onto the bars and the clanging noise rings out. He leans over the hole, peering in. The dead chicken is dangling from his fingers. I hear a creak as the metal gives.

"Watch out," I shout.

My dad yells out something, and the chicken splashes into the water.

FOURTEEN

I'm not the sort of person who hides behind the cushion in the scary bits. I have to see what's happening. You're never going to escape the aliens if you've got your eyes closed.

So I watch as the wobbly bar finally gives way and my dad falls heavily, his body straddling the open hatch. There is the sound of water crashing. I see a dark shape propel out of the water and my stomach turns inside out. I see the silhouette of massive jaws opening. The water boils and I am soaked as the creature smashes back down into the foam.

Then, to my amazement, there is a thud as my dad lands in the brambles next to the cage. How did he manage that? Sneaky bugger.

I'm so relieved I can't speak.

Dad looks like he's winded, clutching his stomach. He'll be all right.

I take a small step towards the cage. The Beast is thrashing around in there. I bet he's angry he missed. I fall back. He looks bigger than ever. The loose bar is now bent down into the cage, close to the surface of the water. There's a big gap in the roof of the cage. I look at the animal inside. Can he get out?

My dad crawls right past me and flops against a tree trunk and sits there gasping. Even through all the facial hair, I can see he's gone pale. I think he's having some kind of panic attack. There's a dribble of white stuff leaking from the corner of his mouth and a cut on his forehead. But what I'm worried about is how I'm going to fix the cage. Could I borrow Eric's welder for a night? Would he notice? Not that I know how to work the thing yet.

Dad grabs a bottle from his pocket and swigs. I wonder if he is having a heart attack. It wouldn't surprise me. He hasn't exactly had a healthy lifestyle. Does booze rot your arteries?

I have this mad urge to look right inside the cage and see what my boy is doing. He's gone so quiet I'm worried he's up to something. I creep over, prepared to leg it if I have to.

He is floating on the surface, his massive head turned towards me. We eyeball each other. A pair of white ridges run down the center of his snout between his eyes. A couple of gray feathers stick out from his jaws.

"Sorry, boy," I whisper. His eyes are black with a gray slit. He is not moving but his eyes are watching me as I move around the cage.

I look up at the broken bar and the open hatch.

This is it, I think to myself.

Have you ever had a nightmare, and when you wake up it doesn't sink in for at least a few minutes that it isn't real? And even after you realize you are lying in your own comfy bed, you are so shit-scared you can't move? You know it's irrational but you lie there, as still as possible, hoping that the evil will pass over you. I feel like that now. I've had nightmares about this. About him escaping. About him following me everywhere I go. If he gets out I'll never be able to go out alone again. And never after dark. And never near deep water. He knows my scent. He connects me with food. He'll track me down one day.

I smell my father coming up behind me. He is breathing fast, horrible, wheezy breaths. I wonder what he's thinking.

"Are you going to get me a gun now?" I ask. To my surprise, my dad claps me on the shoulder.

"Are you mad? He's worth a bloody fortune."

I feel tired. I want to go home. I want to go back and annoy Carol and see what Robert is up to. I don't want to be here, stuck between my gross old dad and a killer reptile.

"Stephen," pants my dad. He jigs up and down. His eyes flicker from me to the cage. "Let me sell him for you. We'll be laughing."

"Who'd want to buy that?" I ask. "A zoo?"

I think my dad smells worse when he's wound up.

He taps the side of his nose. "I got contacts who'd go mad for this."

I can't think of anyone who would want him. Not unless they're thinking of suicide. Crazy old man.

My dad leans close to me and his beard scratches my ear.

"Fighting," he whispers, his breath stinking of alcohol. "Imagine him against a pack of twenty pit bulls."

This is the wrong thing to say to me.

"Is this what you're intending to do with Malackie?" I ask.

My dad susses I am not happy.

"A grizzly bear, then," he says, pulling at his beard. He can't keep still. "Or a pond rammed full of piranha."

111

"You're disgusting," I say. Why did I bring him here? I must be mad.

My father puts his hand on my shoulder and guides me away from the cage. He seems to have forgotten about his injured ankle.

"We'd get twenty grand for him," he says. "We can split it. Don't tell me you don't need the money."

I reckon the Beast can sense what we're talking about because he starts hissing gently.

"They can climb trees, you know," says my dad. "Bloody trees!"

It begins to drizzle rain, and we just stare at each other. My bad tooth starts buzzing. I'd thought it was better. Then there is a sound that sends a chill over me. It starts off quiet, then gets louder. It's a noise I have heard in my worst dreams. A dull *thump, thump, thump,* the sound of thick skin on metal. I turn back to the cage. My boy has pulled himself up to the highest ledge and has grabbed a bar with his jaws. He twists his body back and forth, back and forth, smashing into the bars with his tail. His snout is sticking right out of the cage. I could touch him if I wanted. I've never seen so much of him out of the water before. I'm surprised how dark and rough-looking he is, almost black with green flecks of algae and things like little barnacles stuck to his skin.

The joins in the metal don't look secure enough. How old are they? If one bar has rusted through, why shouldn't all the others? He crashes his weight against the metal, over and over. I wonder if he has done this before, maybe countless times. I wonder if the noise can be heard from the path. Probably not, or someone would have come looking to find out what it was.

"Dad," I say, "let's get out of here."

But my father is gazing through the bars.

"Look at that," he breathes. "Look at the size of it."

The neck of the bottle pokes out of my dad's coat pocket. I reach in and pull it out. There is only about a centimeter of brown liquid in the bottom.

FINEST WHISKEY.

Dad grabs it back off me. No wonder he's acting so weird. He's pissed up to his eyeballs. He starts shaking the bars.

"Go on, my son, come and eat me," he shouts.

"Shut up," I say. I have to get my dad out of here. I'm scared, I admit it. If the Beast breaks out, he'll kill us both. We won't have a chance.

"Come on, Dad." I pull at his sleeve. "This is too dangerous."

But he's lost it. He's found his stick from somewhere and pokes it in the cage with these crazy darting movements, jabbing it into the thick flesh.

"Stop it, Dad," I shout, and try to pull the stick away, but my dad swipes me aside like I'm a fly. I was wrong about his strength. I thought I was nearly as tough as him by now. But I'm not. I think the fright has driven him crazy. I sit on the grass. I might just run off and leave them both. If my old man gets eaten alive, who could connect that with me?

BANG BANG BANG

The sound echoes out over the water as the animal smashes against the bars. My dad swigs the last of his whiskey and chucks the bottle at the cage.

"Didn't get me, did you, you bastard? Didn't get your nice fresh meat."

I've seen my dad like this before. Only last time it was in a

113

pub parking lot and he was taunting a couple of blokes. I don't remember why, but I do know he was acting just like this, trying to be the hard man. Me and Selby were waiting by the fence wishing he'd shut up, knowing otherwise we'd all get our heads kicked in.

BANG BANG BANG

One of the uprights has come loose. Has it always been like that? There are some big trees nearby. Apart from that I am surrounded by bracken, grass, and sheep shit. There's no protection.

BANG BANG BANG

My old man has lost it. He's going crazy, jabbing his stick and laughing. I watch him from a distance, but I can't take my eyes away from the loose strut.

A prickly feeling comes over me as I see that another upright is wobbling. No, there's more. Four bars are moving freely at the top of the cage.

BANG BANG BANG

He won't be able to get out, I tell myself. He won't be able to pull apart the bars. They're made of metal.

"Dad, stop it," I shout.

My dad can't stop himself when he's like this. Eventually he or someone gets punched out or the police arrive. But there's no chance of either of those things happening here.

"He's really angry." My voice breaks. I'm freaking.

"I'm teaching him a lesson," my dad pants. "The ugly bastard."

This is the worst thing that could have happened.

BANG BANG

I've heard there are a few words people say just before they die.

1. God.
2. Mum.
3. Shit.

"Shit," I say.

I freeze and my father screams as the Beast slams into the wobbly bars with the entire weight of his body. He's got his head between the bars. It's hideous. Massive, massive jaws. I stop breathing. With a jerky movement he smashes the rest of his body through. He thuds into the bracken. He's done it. He's out. He moves so quickly it's pointless for me to run. I'm crapping myself and I can't move. The size of him takes my breath away. I reckon he's about twelve feet long.

I hear shouting. I don't know if it is me or my dad. The animal moves fast, heading for the water. I can't see anything except him moving over the ground in a dark blur. He runs like a fucking dinosaur, moving from side to side, flattening everything with his massive, thick tail. He climbs over the bank and I am just in time to see him slip over the shingle and into the reservoir.

The water closes over him. I see a dark shape swimming out towards the middle of the lake.

He's gone.

FIFTEEN

Number 11: Age seventeen. Let a man-eating crocodile loose in a reservoir.

I'm driving like a madman.

There's a killer loose in Gruton Reservoir. I know what he can do. I read it on the Internet. He is a *Crocodylus porosus*, an estuarine crocodile. A *pukpuk*. He is also called a saltwater crocodile because he can live in the sea as well as freshwater. He could grow up to eighteen feet and live till he is seventy years old. Soon he will start looking for food. Salties attack by surprising and pouncing on their prey. They'll eat anything. They'll do whatever it takes to survive. I have seen him tear a pig in half. I have seen him lunge for me. I don't reckon he will let himself starve. Even now he might be eyeing a family picnicking on the shore.

I slow the car as I reach a junction. I am weak and my head feels tight and weird. I pull over onto the verge and switch off the engine. I left my dad behind. I couldn't cope with him. I ran off and left him at the lake looking at the water with his mouth open.

I'm so angry I don't think I'll ever want to see him again.

My head clears and I look at my watch. It is five to one. I realize I'm hungry, and I need to eat more than anything else. I start up the car and drive.

Verity gives me the once-over when I come indoors.

"Where have you been?" she asks. "Not at work?"

"Nope," I say. I decide then that I am never going to go back. What is the point of spending my last days of freedom in a stinking meat factory when any minute I'm going to get arrested for illegally owning a dangerous animal, or maybe I'll just get eaten alive? The Dam Man will remember me asking questions about his tooth necklace. The cops will trace me. Whatever happens, I have a very strong sense that time is running out.

"Stephen, are you all right?" Verity plays with the handle of the broom.

"Fine, it's just the drugs. They'll wear off in a minute," I say.

Verity sucks in her breath. She is not amused. She has been different to me since the fire. I mean, it has been proved that I couldn't have done it, but I think, in her heart of hearts, like Jimmy, she holds me responsible.

"There is half a quiche in the fridge," she says. "If you're hungry."

Thank God for Verity. I cut myself a massive slice and eat it with my fingers. It is cold and the cheese is too strong but I bite

117

through peppers and bacon and my mouth waters even as I'm stuffing it in. The pastry tastes of butter and there are chunks of onion and mushroom. I drop crumbs all over the floor.

"Plate," snaps Verity, slamming one down in front of me.

"It is," I say. I ram the last bit of pastry into my mouth. I give her a grin. She has saved my life.

"Stephen," she says, "I've bought you a bag to move your stuff." She fishes behind a chair and brings out a massive rucksack. "I think you'll find it useful."

This time yesterday I probably would have told her where to stick her bag. But now nothing seems to matter. In fact, the sooner I leave this place the better.

"It's lovely," I say, taking it. "I can live in it."

I lie on my bed for the rest of the day. I'm not doing anything. Just thinking and looking at the ceiling. No one disturbs me. I like it this way. But every time I hear the phone ring I tense up. I expect it to be the police or Mindy. But none of the calls are for me. I look at the wallpaper and think about the drawings behind my head. I don't mind them anymore. They're harmless. How could I have let them spook me out for so long? One crazy kid taking out his frustration with a felt tip. My sneaker is lying on its side on the carpet. The sole has a complicated triangular pattern with deep grooves in the rubber. It looks like a crocodile skin. I think I might be getting ill. Maybe the flu or something. I turn over.

I wonder what he's doing now. I imagine his tail sliding through the reeds, his mouth opening to snap at a fish. Maybe he's looking at the bottom of a rowboat. Looking and wondering.

Maybe he gives it a little knock with his snout. Maybe there are some kids inside who have blagged themselves a boat. Maybe the knock is enough to tip them into the water. Maybe, maybe.

I think of my dad. I didn't offer to give him a lift. I just ran. For all I know, the monster could have come right back out of the water and eaten him alive. I hope he likes his meat well-marinated.

Maybe I could leave an anonymous message at the police station. But would anyone take it seriously? I doubt it. The police always mess things up. I'm not going to risk getting involved with them. No way.

I could leave it there, couldn't I? I could leave the Reynoldses' home soon and never come back. I could slip quietly out into the world and never be seen again.

But life is never like that, is it? Things keep happening until you die.

I have to leave my room to take a leak, and Carol comes up to me on the landing. She's holding a school exercise book.

"What's the difference between a crocodile and an alligator?" she asks me.

There's a long silence.

"What?" I grip the banister for support.

"Crocodile, alligator, what's the difference?"

She's perfectly straight-faced.

"Why?"

"It's for school. I thought you might know."

"How should I know?" I push past her and bolt myself in the bathroom. I sit on the toilet and put my head in my hands.

What does she know?

I pick up a bottle of shampoo and read the label. *Leaves your hair soft and manageable.* Who cares? It seems crazy. Everything in here is mad and pointless. The bath mat, the soap. The curled-up calendar that is two months out of date. All these things are so useless, so *small*, compared to the fact that there is a killer on the loose only a few miles away.

A crocodile's jaws taper. Alligators have rounder, snub noses and they can live in colder climates, like North America. By rights, my boy ought to be dead. This country is supposed to be too cold for him. But he's alive, all right.

Crocodiles can't chew. They aren't built that way. What they do is take hold of you and roll and roll and thrash until you start to come apart. Then they swallow big chunks of you whole. So it's not like a shark or a lion, where they'll take bites out of you.

A crocodile will literally tear you apart.

I wake up trembling in the middle of the night. I won't bore you with my nightmares. There are too many of them. I shut my eyes and fall into another.

SIXTEEN

I lie on my bed with a chest of drawers pulled up against the door. I don't want anyone coming in. I'm too freaked out. I've been lying here for about three hours since breakfast, not doing anything, just thinking.

When my boy gets found, the Dam Man is going to work out where his tooth came from. I wish I hadn't asked him about it. He'll remember me.

But there's nothing I can do. The Beast's way too big and dangerous for me to catch. But should I just sit here and wait until he kills somebody? Do I try to make my dad get me a gun? It's his fault the thing escaped anyway. But how do I get close to the Beast without putting myself in danger? How do I kill him without attracting any attention? And how do I get rid of his body? These aren't new thoughts, you know. Even before he escaped I was wondering what I would do with him. But I've never come up with any proper answers. Well, none except the gun.

Remember number ten on my list? Murder.

Because that's what it would be.

I put my pillow over my head. I like it here. It's dark. I can't hear anything. It's warm. My face gets hot.

Something cuts through the silence and makes me jump, causing a spasm in my guts.

"Stephen, telephone," Carol is shouting to me. I sit up and feel dizzy. I move the chest of drawers just enough so I can squeeze through. I walk downstairs acting like Mr. Casual. The telephone is in the kitchen. This is also where most of the family hangs out because there is a small TV and the fridge. This means I get no privacy at all. I never call anyone anyway. I must be the only kid in the whole world who doesn't have a cell phone. I don't see the point of them. Who would I want to talk to?

"Stephen." It's a voice with one hell of a sore throat.

The old bastard is still alive, then.

"What do you want?" I ask. For some reason I'm relieved to hear from him. I look around for Carol, expecting to see her settled at the kitchen table and ready to listen, but she's not here.

"Why'd you leave me?"

I don't bother to reply. I feel weary about the whole thing.

"You've got us in a right mess now, lad."

I like that. I stay silent.

"We're going to have to catch it."

I decide to speak up. "I'm not bothered about him anymore," I lie. "You let him out. You deal with him."

"No, listen," says my father. "I got someone who's going to take it."

"You told someone?"

If someone else knows, it makes it less of a burden on me.

"Stephen, listen. We've got to catch him as soon as we can. He could do someone serious damage."

Does he think I'm stupid?

"We got some ideas. We need a trap and some bait. Live bait."

"You're not using Malackie," I say. I think I hear someone breathing and I look around, expecting to see Carol with a smug grin on her face. But there's no one there except Dudley, who's under the table pretending to be asleep.

"We'll get a sheep," says my father. "But we need a cage."

He says we need to deliver the Beast to this place in Birmingham over the weekend. He also says we're going to get a thousand pounds each.

Eric sounds surprised when I call him. Maybe he thought I wasn't going to come back. Maybe that's true, but I noticed something in his workshop last time that might help me. I go there in the afternoon. I still feel weird, like I'm asleep.

I step into the workshop and see it at once. It's a rectangular metal frame about fourteen feet by four feet, standing against the back wall. Propped against it are panels, like gates.

"My latest project," says Eric, watching me. "It's for my girlfriend's ferrets."

"But it's massive," I say.

"She's got five," he says. "And they need a lot of space. She doesn't have to feel guilty about not giving them enough exercise."

Eric tells me he has to finish welding the panels, then attach chicken wire so they don't escape.

"It's pretty heavy-duty for the job," admits Eric. "But they'd gnaw through wood, and this will last forever."

I like the sound of that. Something that lasts forever.

Eric wipes his hands on his apron and asks me to find his calculator, so I go next door to the office. There are three cash boxes on the shelf — a black one, a red one, and a blue one. They're all locked.

I take the calculator back to Eric. He says he's having a bad day. One of his customers has complained about some rust on a gate he made six years ago. Also he can't get the forge hot enough because the fan isn't working properly. He puts the finishing swirls on a garden gate strut using a gas torch and a pair of pliers.

I spend the afternoon sweeping the floor, and Eric shows me how to use the Linisher machine to make curves in wall brackets. He's impressed how quickly I suss it out. But it's pretty easy, really. Anyone could do it. I like standing with my earphones on in the middle of a shower of sparks. I feel safe in the fire. I like the way that, although the sparks burn so bright and orange, they don't hurt when they land on my skin. It's like magic.

I abandon the meat factory and go down to Eric's every day. After the third day there's a pattern. In the mornings I have to do a load of donkey work, like moving steel rods from the delivery van, carting coal, cleaning the tools, going on deliveries and fittings with him, stuff like that. Sometimes he even makes me walk Dog. I think he only does it to get me out of his face for half an hour. I don't mind. But in the afternoons he lets me help him with metalworking. He has shown me how to do basic welding and I'm helping him put together his girlfriend's ferret cage. If I mess up the welding on a joint, I melt it down and start all over again. My hands have been scorched several times and I've got a heat blister on my thumb. I've set fire to my hair too. Hair burns really fast. I never realized. The fire just pours up your head and you haven't got a chance to do anything. I shaved my head that night. I look a lot like Selby now. Let's hope I don't turn out like him, eh? Carol took one look at my hair and told me I looked a lot better. I didn't know what to say. She is behaving very strangely. She hasn't accused me of nicking anything or tried to wind me up for ages. I expect she's glad I'm leaving.

Eric asks me where I am going after the Reynoldses'. He makes a face when I tell him St. Mark's but doesn't say anything. What he *does* say is that I can keep coming back here even when I'm at St. Mark's.

It's nice to be wanted.

Eric has a radio playing most of the day. More Orchard FM. While he's out of the workshop I turn the radio off. I don't want to hear the news. When I go to buy us cakes, I avoid looking at the headlines on the newspapers. I know it's just a matter of time. And it's all my fault. I realize I ought to try to feed the crocodile. But I haven't got any money to buy meat, and since I left the factory the supply of chickens has run out. Besides, how would I do it? You can't just float a dead pig on the surface of a reservoir.

Have you seen that crazy Australian bloke on the telly? You know, the one who jumps on the back of massive man-eaters and puts his hands over their eyes to calm them down? I could use his help, couldn't I? Hungry Saltie, cruising the waves in an English reservoir? That bloke would be flying over in his helicopter in an instant and take my boy off to some zoo or release him in the wild. I quite like that idea. That's a fantasy. But there is information on this bloke's Web site about how to build a crocodile trap. Can you believe it? Do they seriously think anyone is going to build one? Well, I am grateful anyway. It talks about hinges and doors and bait. It talks about night-vision glasses and the waiting game.

I persuade Eric to put the door of the ferret cage at one end on big hinges. I say it will be easy to attach to a shed or hutch that way. I say it means if one of the ferrets gets ill, his girlfriend can get right in to fetch it out. Eric listens to me. He adapts the cage according to my ideas. I like that.

They have set a day for my transfer to the hostel. Today is Tuesday, Mindy says she'll meet me next Monday in her office, ready to accompany me over to St. Mark's. She's offered to come and pick me up from the Reynoldses' and Jimmy's also said he'll drive me. But I've got my own car. What do I need a lift for? They're probably just trying to make sure I really leave.

Now that they have set a date for my leaving, I look at the house with different eyes.

I sit eating my shepherd's pie with Robert and Carol in front of the telly. It's raining outside. Robert is telling me a joke about a bicycle and a woman's arse. Carol is giving me sneaky looks while she pretends to watch the show. In the kitchen, Jimmy and Verity sit at the table and chat. They've given up trying to make us all sit with them. My room seems different. There's my telly and my Xbox. There's the new rug Verity got for me after Robert tipped over a bottle of ink on the carpet. I can see the garden from the window. The swing moves gently, the rain splashing off the empty seat.

Verity gave me a tenner last autumn to plant five hundred daffodil bulbs, and now they're all coming up. I look at my bed. I wonder who'll sleep in it next. Who will find the drawings behind the headboard? What will the Reynoldses say about me when I'm gone?

On Wednesday I go to see Eric. We work more on the cage.

Eric says he has to go out this morning but I'm welcome to stay and work "as long as you don't set the place on fire." I give him a look when he says that. I wonder if he's referring to the village hall. But he looks miles away. He's tense, distracted.

I'm having trouble with the cage. I've got to join three bits of metal together and there isn't enough space. I turn off the radio so I can concentrate better. I remember there's new set of welding rods in the office, so I go in to get them. The red cash box is wide open on the desk. It is stuffed full of twenties. I look around. Dog wags at me from his basket.

Eric isn't exactly rich, but he has enough. He rents a big house on the outskirts of town. He's got his truck and is saving up to go snowboarding with his mates in Canada. I look at the money. How handy would a couple of those notes be? The temptation is killing me. But Eric has been cool with me. I pick up the wad of money. I feel the thickness of the bundle and listen to the crackle of paper. He wouldn't miss one or two, would he? Something catches my eye in the bottom of the tin. It's a plastic key ring. It has a picture of a pirate on it and says Jamaica Inn.

The spare keys to Eric's truck.

So you'll be pleased to hear that I don't steal one penny from Eric. I put the money back, collect the welding rods, and return to work on my cage.

No, I don't nick the cash. It feels too tight. Eric is all right. It would be like thieving from your mate.

This doesn't stop me from borrowing his truck.

SEVENTEEN

I have a weakness for cars, all sorts. I like sporty ones, classics, especially Jags. I even like new stuff that most people hate. Like BMW minis and the new VW Beetle. I'd love to nick one of those Smart cars. Just to see how fast it would go. Selby would be up for that. Me and him used to fix ourselves up with something on a Friday night, hot-wire it and floor the hell out of it, just to see how fast it would go. There's this road outside town. It's really straight, and one night me and Selby got up to 113 mph in this Peugeot 305. Brilliant. Selby was driving, of course. I hardly ever got to drive. He's five years older than me.

We didn't get caught that night. Actually we didn't get caught most nights. Selby is a good driver. We kept our heads down — until we reached the straight, that is.

A lot of kids we know, they'd burn the car out when they'd finished with it. Me and Selby did that a couple of times, but after a while it felt like a waste. I like cars too much to burn them. I like French cars best. That's why I've got me this old Renault 5.

It's not the flashiest ride, but it's reliable. Sound like an old man, don't I?

Eric drives this flatbed Bedford truck. It's pretty shit. It's only got four gears. Can you believe it? But it's the only way I can think of to get the cage to the reservoir.

I'm painting the main frame of the cage with black metallic paint when Eric comes back. He's got me a burger, a can of Coke, and some fries.

"It's coming along," he says, settling into a wheelbarrow full of rubbish to eat his lunch. He swings his legs. I think he's amused. "Never seen a ferret cage like it, though."

He sniggers and pings the wet metal. "I hope she likes it, 'cos it's going to last a very, very long time."

I wonder why he's in such a good mood. This morning he was pretty uptight.

He takes a massive bite of his burger and leans over to examine the joints on the cage. The effort nearly topples him out of the wheelbarrow.

"You've gotten pretty good at this," he says.

I am so surprised I stop painting. I thought I'd messed it all right up. There are dribbles of dried metal everywhere and untidy bulges.

"Thanks," I say. I feel embarrassed and move round to paint the other side.

"Want to learn more?" he asks. "And get paid for it?"

"Eh?" I stop working and turn to face him.

"I've been to the bank this morning," he says. "And they've approved my loan. I can afford to take someone on, part-time. Interested?"

I don't know what to say. I just stand and look at him,

running my fingers over the serrated edges of his truck keys in my pocket.

"I can give you six pounds an hour to start with. It can go up once you've been here a few months and learned a few things." Eric climbs out of the wheelbarrow, balls his burger wrapper, and chucks it at the bin. "Twenty hours a week. I know it's not much, but it's all I can afford at the moment." He looks at me quizzically. "So?"

"Yeah," I say. I grin. "Thanks."

Stupid bugger, aren't I? As if he's going to hire me after I nick his truck.

Later, I drive to the reservoir parking lot. I sit in my car a long time before I finally get out. The evenings are getting lighter now but low fog hangs over the water. My boy could be anywhere, behind that hedge, underneath that scrub. He could be just beneath the surface of the water. It's been six days since he broke out and there's been nothing on the news: no stories of missing fishermen or decapitated walkers, no sightings of crocodiles lying on the banks. There's a small, hungry part of me that hopes he's died and that the shock of his new territory has finished him off. But I know this is wishful thinking.

I walk out over the dam and look into the deep water. A line of buoys bobs on the surface. I feel safer up here. There is a fifteen-foot drop and a wall of concrete between me and him. But I know he's under there somewhere, watching and waiting. I know he's growing hungry.

There are footsteps behind me.

"We're closing," says a voice. It's the Dam Man. Not again. I can't believe it. Why is he suddenly here all the time? He looks at me curiously. "Well, if it isn't Danny Slater," he says. He sounds sarcastic, and I nod at him and turn back to the water.

"Have you lost something?" The Dam Man leans his elbows next to mine. "Where's that dog of yours?"

I shrug. "Gave him away," I say.

The Dam Man sighs.

"There have been some funny-looking blokes hanging around here recently," he says. "Not from around here. You ought to look out for yourself."

I wonder if he is referring to my father. Has he been back?

"I don't suppose you know anything about them?" he asks.

I shake my head. "I've got to go," I say.

But I don't drive home. Instead I park the car in the pull-off farther up the road and crawl through the hedge. I walk down through the field. It's getting pretty dark now. Crocodiles hunt at night. If I had any sense, I would get in the car and go home. But something is making me go on. I have to see the broken water cage to make it sink in that it really has happened and that he really has escaped. In the field before the fence I crouch in the wet grass and give myself a few minutes. The air smells different, like clothes drying over a radiator. It's April. The water in the reservoir will be warming up. I nearly shit myself when I see something large and dark move at the bottom of the field. But it's quickly followed by another shape. I shine my flashlight and realize it's cows. They haven't been here all winter.

I'm sure I've seen a wildlife program on the telly where all these crocs lie in wait in the watering hole, and when the buffalo or whatever comes to drink, *wham!* The croc lunges. I remind myself there's a six-foot metal fence between me and the water.

I think he knows my smell. If he is anywhere near, he might know I am coming. And what is worse is that he associates me with food. Correction. He associates anything with blood in it with food.

It's harder than usual to climb over the fence. How the hell did I do it with a bag of meat each time? I sit at the top for a long time, the metal links cutting through my jeans. It feels safe up here. I should have a rope handy next time, just in case I need to make a quick getaway. I drop to the ground and crunch through the dead bracken. I bet he can hear every step. Why didn't my dad get me a gun? He cares more about making money than his own son's life. Selby would love this. I can imagine him walking ahead; he always has to be in front. He would have a weapon — a machete or a shotgun or something. He wouldn't come out here empty-handed. Not like me. He would be making too much noise. He'd be swearing under his breath and cracking jokes to hide his nerves. He'd be stomping down plants and snapping branches off trees.

I reach the path. "Shut it, Selb," I whisper, stepping over it. It's really dark and wet down here. My flashlight makes this pathetic little line of light. But I know where I'm going. I have walked down here in blackness hundreds of times. Only tonight it feels different. Every few paces I find I am stopping and listening. I'm expecting to hear twigs popping followed by a deep growl. But there is nothing but the wind over the water and my own heavy breathing. I hear a high-pitched squeaking and something tiny flies at me out of the sky and dips away. Bats. They've got them at the Reynoldses' too. Carol doesn't believe I can hear them. She says the noise they make is too high-pitched for the human ear. But like now, sometimes I hear this sound, a bit like rubbing wet glass with your finger, and sure enough, sooner or later this little monster comes swooping out of the sky.

Frogs, they make a noise too. I'm not talking about croaking. They scream. It's a horrible noise. I've only heard it once. It was because Dudley had hold of it. I heard the screaming and had to see what was going on. I booted Dudley out of the way, lucky no one saw, and grabbed the frog. But it moved too quickly and it was out of my hands before I could get hold of it. It slipped into a crack in the wall. I expect everything will scream when it's in danger. I wonder what noise I'll make when the Beast gets me in his jaws. Will I have time to scream before the death roll?

I'm at the cage. Two bars have broken off completely and lie in the grass. I shine the beam into the water. It is still and black. It's true. He *has* escaped. It wasn't a dream. He is out here somewhere. I switch off the flashlight, reckoning that it doesn't really help me to see, but it will sure as hell lead him to me. I don't know what to do now. It's too scary to be out here on my own. I don't want to be reptile food. Leaving the cage behind, I poke about in the place where I last saw him running down over the bank. There is nothing moving on the shoreline. Nothing coming towards me. If I stay away from the water I should be all right.

There's a dark hump on the stones. I can't make out what it is, but it's still. It could possibly be a large animal. I would have to go closer to see for sure. Now that I've seen it, I don't want to turn my back on it in case it does turn out to be something. The flashlight isn't any help. I force myself to take a step and then another. No, it's still not moving. I am walking above it, so it's between me and the water. I'm not going to take any chances. A few more paces and I realize I have been freaking out over a tree stump. He could be anywhere. He could be on the other side of the lake by now. He might have left it altogether. Even now he could be munching all the goldfish in someone's pond.

I don't know why I'm thinking all this. I know full well he's probably only a few feet away from me. Just waiting to make his move. The ground gets steep and slippery and I smell something really bad.

It's a severed sheep's head. There's no sign of the body. A purple tongue hangs out of the mouth. I step back and my feet shoot out from under me as I fall over. I land flat on my arse in a slick of mud. As I get up I can see a dim pathway of mud leading to the reservoir. It's wet, as if something big has recently crawled out of water.

I'm going home now. I have found out what I need to know. He's still here.

EIGHTEEN

On Friday morning I'm eating my breakfast of fried eggs, sausages, and baked beans when Robert comes in and sits opposite me. He's wearing a T-shirt with a cartoon of a woman wearing nothing but a motorbike helmet and biker gloves.

"When are you going, then?" he asks.

"Monday," I say. And I feel depressed.

Robert works at a hole in the plastic tablecloth with his penknife. "Can I come and visit you?" he asks.

I don't know what to say.

I have only seen the outside of St. Mark's. It's a converted warehouse near the center of town. The shape of it and the rows of rectangular windows make it look like a prison. There's a massive cobbled courtyard in front with a disused concrete fountain that's full of scummy water. It's in the area you always hear about in the news, where there's been a stabbing or a drug raid. I don't think Robert would like it much.

"We can meet in town," I say. "Go for a burger."

"Cool," Robert says, picking at his scab. Then he stands up so quickly he knocks his chair over.

"I'm staying over at Jerome's this weekend," he says.

"So it's good-bye, then," I say.

"Yeah."

"See you later."

He's not going to visit me. Verity would never let him. I don't think he has even been on the bus to town on his own yet. I push my breakfast away.

Suddenly I don't feel like eating.

My dad phones in the middle of the afternoon. It's a shock to hear from him, even now. He's not slurring his words or talking shit. He's obsessed with making some money out of this. I haven't allowed myself to think too much about what he intends to do. It's too sick.

"So?" he asks me. "Have you sorted out a vehicle?"

"Yeah," I say. "And I've got a cage."

"Good lad." My dad sounds surprised. "I've got the bait."

I dread to think what that is. He tells me to get some wire cutters and strong rope.

I tell him I won't do anything unless he promises not to be pissed. To my surprise he agrees. We arrange to meet at eleven p.m.

Eric's truck sits half on the pavement just outside his house. At a quarter to ten I'm parked in a side street and am working myself up. The lights are still on in his living room but the curtains are closed. That helps.

I'm trying not to think about what happens next, I mean after tonight. I've been arrested for nicking cars before, and I'm still here, aren't I? I'll work out what to do about Eric tomorrow. Right now, I've got a big man-eater to worry about.

The moon is half out. This is good. It will give us light, but not too much.

A man walks past with his dog. He eyes me quickly and walks on. When he has gone, I step quietly up to Eric's truck. My hands feel like they belong to someone else. I watch one as it slides the spare key into the hole and twists. I hear the spring pop and the latch go up. My other hand grips the handle and opens the door. There is a creak, and I freeze. But the light keeps flickering behind Eric's curtains. He's probably watching some DVD with his girlfriend. I climb up into the driver's seat and gently close the door. It has caught but is not shut properly. I'll give it a good slam when I'm on my way. Maybe, just maybe, I'll be able to do all of this without Eric realizing. Who am I trying to kid? I'll never catch a crocodile, drive it to Birmingham, and have the truck back here before he realizes it's missing. I'm in deep shit which-ever way I look at it.

The key slips into the ignition and it starts first time. I don't look at the house. I pull into first and drive gently off the curb. When I'm on the road I try to stay calm. I don't want to go too fast. I don't want to draw attention to myself.

I left a side door unbolted at Eric's workshop this afternoon. Lucky no chancer found it, eh? I switch on the light. I feel like a stranger here now. I can see the hammer I've been using and my gloves on the bench, but they belong to somebody else now. I'll never wear them again. I breathe in the rich smoky smell.

I know it's going to be a hell of a job dragging the cage out of the double doors and getting it to the truck. It's bloody heavy. But while I was making it I knew I'd have to do this on my own, so I encouraged Eric to make both side panels detachable so it would be easier for me to manage. Now I've unscrewed the panels so they lie on the concrete floor while I'm pulling the frame out of the doors. It scrapes over the ground. I try to lift it but can only manage a few feet before my arms go dead. I open the truck doors and grab one end of the cage. I am edging onto the back of the truck when something flies out past me and scampers into the workshop. It's Dog. He must have been asleep in the truck. I'm so surprised I drop the cage and it lands on my foot. Pure slapstick. Har bloody har. Only I'm not laughing. I can't even swear in case someone hears me. At least my foot deadened the sound of the fall. I try to ignore the pain and summon all my strength to lift the frame into the truck. It fits. Thank God. I go back for the panels and Dog trots at my heels. He isn't aware that I've pissed all over his boss by nicking his truck and breaking into his workshop. Dog thinks this is wicked. A nighttime adventure.

I don't want to think about how Eric is going to feel when he finds that his truck and his dog are missing. I feel like a right shit. I leave Dog locked in the workshop. He'll be a lot safer there than where I'm going.

Eric's truck is a bastard to drive. I can't stop crunching the gears, and the brakes are shot to pieces. I feel safer when I've left the town, too many coppers about. But even on the country roads I freeze up when headlights go past. I really, really don't want to get stopped. Somehow I manage the twenty-odd miles out to the reservoir. It's nearly midnight when I get to the pull-off. I park behind a bush and turn the lights off.

I wait in the darkness.

There is a knock on the window that makes me jump out of my seat.

Most people look better in the dark — how can they not? But my dad looks like something that has crawled out of a grave. His beard is wilder than ever and his hair makes this horrible helmet shape round his head. His eyes look black, with no light in them. The moonlight exaggerates all his worst features — the bulgy piss head nose, the cut-off chin, and the big yellow teeth.

"Where the hell have you been?" he asks as I wind down the window.

I like that. I've managed to build a cage and find a truck. I've got wire cutters, rope, a kitchen knife, and three blankets. And he's standing there mouthing off at me. But at least he seems sober. I had my doubts.

"Where's the bait, then?" I ask. "Still eating grass?"

He holds out a bag. There is a muffled squawk.

"Chicken?" I say. "He'll like that." I don't want to know where he got it from.

"Really we should get us a lamb," says my dad, leaning into the window. I am engulfed in his stale breath. It makes me want to retch. But at least he doesn't stink of alcohol, not yet. "And cut it so it bleeds slowly and skips around, *baaa*ing for its ma."

I wind up the window and get out, roughly pushing him aside.

"Stop messing around," I say.

We find a gate and drive down through the field. The ground is wet and we'll be leaving tire tracks, but I can't think about that now. I only hope we don't get bogged in. We have to leave the truck by the fence. It will be a hell of a job dragging the cage back up when it's full, but I reckon it's possible. My dad insists on cutting the fence himself, and he takes ages trying to get a perfect rectangular hole. I sit on the cage and watch him sever each wire link in turn. The fence gradually slackens and he twangs the wire. I think he's enjoying himself. But then he moans all the way to the water even though he's only carrying the frame. I'm carrying two panels and I've got the front end of the frame, which is always the heaviest. My dad's puffing and blowing like an old woman. I won't let myself get like him, ever.

The half-moon shines on the water. Nothing moves. The trees are still and the water is smooth. The visibility is good. Too good. Right now, he might be swimming around, hunting. Who knows where he is? A different mood has come over my dad. He's no longer cracking sick jokes or taking the piss but struggles to bolt the panels together. I could do it in minutes but I don't want to get too close to the water. My dad has taken control now. He orders me to fetch the other spanner and I do, obedient as a dog.

I'd be lying if I said I'm not scared. I'm terrified. I've looked after this thing for years and it's not like any other animal. You know, like, with a dog or a cat you can get a kind of bond. They'll understand what you mean, up to a point. People can train almost any sort of animal. But you can never train a crocodile. They have only one instinct, and that is survival.

In the past, lying on the bars and looking into the water I've had the feeling that I was looking at something totally alien to me. Something that doesn't belong in the modern world. Next time you see a picture of a crocodile, just look into its eyes. You'll be looking at a dinosaur.

The moon is higher in the sky and a plane flies over. Its red lights flash like a spaceship. I have an urge to run. To get back in the van, take it back to Eric, get my car back, and go back to the Reynoldses'. At least I'm physically safe there. Out here I'm a sitting target. The Beast could be anywhere.

"Stephen!" shouts my dad, far too loud. "Give me a hand."

I slide over the mud to the cage. My sneakers are filthy and the wet is beginning to sink through to my skin. I roll up my jeans so they don't get covered. I stand at the back, as far from the water as possible, but I can't stop staring, imaging I can see pinpricks of light beneath the surface. Pinpricks that might be the eyes of a hungry killer.

We don't talk much. I want to be able to hear everything, and every crack in the bushes behind, every splash from a jumping fish, makes me want to scream. My breathing sounds too loud. I bet someone could hear it from the other side of the lake. As for my dad, with his stink and his swearing he might as well light a fire to announce our presence. I feel afraid of everything — every bird that flies past, every car that goes by up on the road. Everything is a threat. Everything is against me.

The cage is finally built. I tie my rope to the door panel and pull it open. I have no idea if this will work but I don't have a choice. I don't know how to trap crocodiles, do I? I've only read about it on the Internet. My dad grabs the chicken out of the bag. Its legs are tied together but it flaps and flaps and squawks a little. He throws it to the back of the cage and it flops around on the bars in the mud.

And I think *I'm* having a crap time!

Now the bit I've really been dreading. At a nod from my dad, we push the cage a little way into the water so that it is half submerged. I skip back from the water as soon as I can and tie a second rope to the base of the cage. We trail the rope over the shingle back to the bushes. I check behind me carefully and decide that I will be safest if I have my back to a tree. I settle into the grass; my arse gets soaked immediately but I don't care. This whole thing is a nightmare. My dad ties the base rope to the tree and flops next to me. He checks that I'm holding the rope that holds open the door and he grunts.

"I got the address," he says. "We got plenty of time."

I haven't got plenty of time. I have this little hope that we'll do the whole job tonight. But maybe things will go exactly according to plan. The beast will smell out the chicken, crawl in the cage, and I'll let go of the rope holding the door open. Then we'll drag it back up to the truck, take it to Birmingham, be paid a thousand pounds each, and be home by morning. I'll spend my money on the first few months' rent for a nice flat and I'll work for Eric. He'll never know the truck was missing.

Don't laugh, I told you it was a small hope.

But this ought to work. The Beast must be hungry. He's never hunted in his life, he doesn't know how to feed himself. If I was him I would hang around in the usual place waiting for me to come along with a hundredweight of pork.

I'm getting cold now, and the wet is beginning to piss me off. I grab a handful of ferns to sit on. I think my dad has nodded off. He's making these horrible snoring noises anyway. You'd think he'd be scared, wouldn't you? Maybe this is all just a big laugh to him. His head drifts onto my shoulder and I push it off and move away. I sit for ages and nothing happens. I get pins and needles in my foot and have to walk around a bit. The wind has gotten up and waves lap around the cage. The night seems to be getting darker. The chicken doesn't seem to be moving, and I wonder if it's died of shock. I realize that there is a good chance we won't catch him tonight. I don't want to think what I'll do if that is the case. I look at the stars. Some are brighter than others. I don't know the names of any of them. Who cares anyway? There are big clouds drifting across the sky. Slowly they knock out the stars and the moon and it gets even darker. I check my watch: 2:15 a.m. I've been here for two hours and nothing is happening. I reckon I have, at the most, four hours left. My dad is definitely asleep now. He's breathing out through his mouth and making all these horrible snorting noises. I wish Selby was here. He'd know what to do. I'd love to call him up and tell him to come and help. He'd be well up for it. He'd love it. He'd be swimming the lake with a snorkel and a flashlight looking for the bugger. Gran says Selby doesn't have any sense. It's not true. He just doesn't have any fear. I wonder how long you can be scared for. I've been on edge for hours now. My guts have turned to liquid. How long before I do myself an injury? I wonder what it's like for some prisoner in a cell. Somewhere where they allow torture. You'd be scared every second of every day. Can you die of fear?

I shouldn't have fed him so much. I should have done more reading on the Internet. He's grown way too fast. He expects too much food. I should have left him to die in my dad's lockup. He's been my biggest worry for years. All the shit, all the foster homes, all the trouble I've been in, it's nothing compared to this, is it? I think of Selby. Maybe it's not the worst thing.

I'm leaning against the tree. My legs have gone dead. It seems like hours later. Nothing is happening at the cage. I am beginning to think we should give up and go home. My dad got up and had a piss about half an hour ago. Then came back and went right off to sleep again. I look down at him. He's used to sleeping outdoors. This is just home away from home for him. I got tired of holding the rope hours ago, so I've tied it to a low branch. I've got my knife handy so when he goes in the cage, I can slash the rope and *bang!* The lid will fall down. Easy-peasy. Easy-peasy. God, I'm knackered. I'm still waiting. I've been waiting for hours. It is still very, very dark. And it's so cold I'm tempted to sit next to my dad to get some of his warmth, but I never would, you know that. It's spring, for God's sake. It's supposed to be warming up. This is like the North Pole or something. I'll probably die of exposure.

I'm dozing off when I think I hear a crackle behind me. I tell myself it's a squirrel or something and allow my eyes to close. There are more noises. Like something is being dragged through the grass. I make myself open my eyes. I know it's nothing to worry about, maybe a badger. All the same, I'm not just going to sit here.

Then I'm completely awake. Dad's not here. Where's he gone?

Something is coming towards me, very slowly. I can't move. I'm too cold. I just keep still and listen. There is the sound of air coming out through a small space.

I know it's the Beast. It has to be. But I can't move. Some part of me is fooling myself that if I stay very still, he won't find me.

"Dad?" I say quietly. A twig snaps behind me.

I don't know where to run. I don't want to go near the water, that would mean certain death, but I can't go back either, because that's where he is. I wonder if I can climb up the tree. I start to move my foot when something comes out into the clearing.

"Fuck," I gasp.

"Quiet, for God's sake," whispers a terrified voice. "It's just over there. It's watching us."

"What?"

"Stay still, he's stalking us."

It's Carol.

NINETEEN

She's wearing a hood and her face is in deep shadow. She puts her hand on mine. It's shaking. To say I'm shocked would be an understatement.

"See?" She nods at a clump of brambles to my right. I look harder. All I can see is a long moon shadow. Then I recognize the shape. It's an open jaw and my shadow is sitting right inside it. Then I see the real thing.

He is lying close to the ground, deadly still. I see his head and massive jaw. The rest of his body is hidden in brambles. He's staring right at me and is only about twelve feet away. I stare, unable to move or decide what to do next. I'm going to die.

"I don't think he knows we can see him," whispers Carol. "We've got a chance."

I can't drag my eyes away. He just gazes calmly at me, like he's hypnotizing me. The mouth closes as slow as dust falling.

He could lunge any second. I've seen how fast he can move. Much faster than me. If I want to have any chance of survival I have to run. Now. But I can't. I want to move. It feels like every cell in my body is tingling. But I can't move my legs. Could I climb the tree? Would I make it? How long has he been there? Why is he just watching me? If I stay still, maybe he won't go for me.

I have to move. I'll do it in just a minute. I'll move very, very slowly behind the tree. I'll move so slowly he won't notice. Who am I fooling? He has night vision, for God's sake. He can see everything.

Something's happening. That's it. I am moving my foot, so, so slowly. It has nearly gone dead from sitting still for so long. It has to hold me up. Slowly I pull my feet up under me. Oh, God, it twitched its head. That head. It really is a dinosaur. It knows I'm moving.

Oh, God. He's coming for me. I'm on my feet and moving back, he's moving incredibly fast. He's lunging for me. He's propelling at me. I'm behind a tree. Oh, God, he really does want to kill me. He's coming again. His back is massive, he's flattening everything. I can't climb this tree. He's coming round for me.

"Stephen!" Carol screams.

The Beast is still. He's watching me. He's going to come any se —

Oh!

I see a tree I can climb. I sprint towards it and yank Carol after me. I don't think he expected me to go this way, but he's moving again and he's fast. I nearly trip but I save myself. We're at the tree. The Beast has grabbed something on the ground. He thinks it's me. I'm lifting Carol up to the lowest branch, she's scrabbling and kicking my back and shoulders. Damn, he's dropped it. What is it? My rucksack. I'm climbing up behind

Carol, who's pulling me up by my collar. She climbs the tree like a bloody monkey. He's beneath me. He's going to rear up and rip my legs off. I'm pulling myself up with the bones of my fingers. I'm tearing my fingernails, digging them into the bark. Carol is making a noise. She's giving me her hand. I have to take it. There's a strong branch just above me. I have to get my leg over it.

He's coming.

Whoa!

My foot. I feel something on my foot.

He's gone down again.

I'm all right.

We're safe. He can't reach us unless he really does know how to climb trees.

He waits.

I open my eyes. I don't know how long I've had them shut but it seems that I've been listening to the snorting, the growls, the crack of branches below, for hours and hours. I sit in the fork between two broad branches. My feet are tightly drawn up. I think I'm safe here. He pounces, propelling his body high into the air. I hear his teeth knock together as his jaws shut. I feel the draft.

But he hasn't got me. Not yet.

I hear Carol breathing. She is higher than me. Her feet are close to my head. She says nothing.

I force myself to look down. He's prowling around the foot of the tree, he's lying still, he's getting up again. He's guarding the tree. There's no way we can get down safely. I wish I had a gun.

"Oh, God."

I force myself to look away from the crocodile and up at Carol. One of her feet is dangling in the air.

"You all right?" My voice doesn't sound like mine. It's as thick and rasping as my dad's.

"No," Carol says. She starts coughing, which turns into sobbing. She shifts and the whole tree wobbles. I cling to the trunk. My hearing is going and my head feels fuzzy, like I'm wasted. I'm going to fall. My fingers are going to lose their grip. I'm going to be ripped into pieces by those horrible teeth. This is the end of me. This is what it's like.

"Selby," I whisper.

I try to get a better grip on the tree. It's like being on a fairground ride when you think you're going to fall out of the safety harness. I look up at Carol. Behind her dark outline the sky is getting lighter.

"I've got some chocolate," she says in a small voice.

But in order to take it I'll have to move one of my hands, and they're both holding me on the tree.

"Do you think we're safe?" Carol hands me down a square of chocolate. I drop it. For a dizzy moment I think I'm going to topple after it.

"I'm going to start shouting for help as soon as it gets to five o'clock," she says. "There might be a farmer up or someone who can help us."

"No," I whisper. "They'll get killed."

We fall silent as the Beast paces over the ground, its tail dragging behind. I think I can smell it — a sour, dark smell, like

150

rotten oil or blood. I hear it breathing, like air escaping from a tire.

Carol passes me more chocolate. This time I don't drop it, and the creamy sweet taste spreads over my tongue. I wriggle my fingers to see if they work and let out my breath. My head is clearing. I'm not going to fall.

I was only minutes from sleep, down at the foot of the tree. I'd be dead if it wasn't for Carol.

"I'm cold," she says. "Is there enough room for me down there?"

I can't move. I will fall. But she has already begun to lower herself from her branch. Her foot fumbles for a hold so I take her ankle and guide it to a branch. She lets herself down slowly and wedges in next to me.

"That's better," she says. She is so close her hair is tickling my nose. It smells of perfume. I feel the warmth coming from her body.

We sit in silence, watching the crocodile watching us. He's lying on his belly, not moving and being very quiet. Maybe he thinks he's going to fool us, make us believe he's gone away. I preferred it when he was moving about. Now that he is still, I have no idea what he's going to do next.

"They hunt at night," I say. "Maybe he'll go in the morning."

Carol has gone quiet. This might sound mad to you, but it is only now, when the dawn is coming and Carol is snuggled up against me, that I wonder what she's doing here.

I draw a breath to ask her when she begins to speak.

"I've known you've been up to something for ages," she says. Her voice is almost back to normal but there is something strained in it. "After that pig. I didn't believe it was for your dad."

I swallow. Dad. There was no screaming. He might have gotten away. He might have abandoned me hours ago. I'm not going to think about him right now.

"I've followed you a couple of times," she says. "I knew you were keeping something here. I knew it was big and it was in that cage. I heard you talking to your dad on the phone and I followed you out here last week. I saw it escape."

She must have come on her bloody moped.

I'm speechless. Everything is lost now. But deep down I'm not really surprised. Carol is the sneakiest person I know.

"I think it's incredible," she says. "But now I wish I'd told someone."

"Is that what the alligator question was about?" I ask.

She grins. "Did I freak you out?"

I should have been more careful. It's light enough that I can make out the chicken in the cage, now lying still in the mud. I wonder if it's still alive. I wish it would wake up and start flapping around to distract him.

Carol shuffles to make herself comfortable and digs her elbow into my side.

"I thought as long as you kept quiet about the village hall, I wouldn't say anything about you," she tells me. "You seemed to have things under control."

"Yeah, right," I say. I can't believe we're up here having this conversation.

I notice a line of pink light on the horizon.

"Stephen," asks Carol, "who's Selby?"

A pause.

"My brother," I say. "He's dead."

"Oh," she says.

We are both quiet for a long time after that.

I don't think I doze off. I'm too scared of falling out of the tree but somehow it's daylight and I'm dying for a piss. Carol's arms are wrapped around the tree trunk and she isn't making a sound.

I look down. I can't see him. Has he gone? I look hopefully at the cage but it's empty apart from the chicken, which, in addition to coming back to life, has managed to get the string off its feet and is pecking around in the water. But where is my Beast?

There's also no sign of my dad. A heavy mass heaves in my stomach. *One thing at a time*, I tell myself. *Put him out of your mind.*

"Carol, wake up." I nudge her and have to grab her to stop her from falling.

"What?" She opens her eyes and looks really puzzled.

I look at the water, at the bushes, at the stretch of shingle, and through the trees behind.

He's gone.

If I stay up here any longer I'll piss myself. I have to get down or I'll have to do it in front of Carol. I climb down. I'm stiff and aching all over. My back is killing me right at the bottom of the spine.

The ground feels soft and wet. I look up at Carol who waits to see if I get eaten before she lowers herself down.

"What's that?"

There's rustling in the brambles by my feet. A rabbit legs it out over the grass. When I can breathe again I start wondering what to do next. I don't know what to say to Carol. It's funny that after spending hours and hours wedged together, neither of us can look at each other.

"So," says Carol, "what's the plan?"

I can't believe it. Is she giving me a choice? I thought she'd be running to the police as soon as she could.

"I don't know."

"I assume," she says carefully looking around her, "that you wanted to catch this thing and take it somewhere. Birmingham? Am I right?"

She really *has* been listening to my telephone calls.

I nod.

"And you don't want anyone to know you've been keeping him here?"

"That's right," I say, aware that I am completely at her mercy.

"Then we need to hide the cage until tonight," she says.

I am stunned.

"Carol," I say, "there is a twelve-foot man-eating crocodile on the loose. It wants to kill us. It will kill anything."

"I know," she says. Though she looks tired, her eyes are shining.

Why aren't you scared? She almost looks like she's enjoying herself.

"I'll help you," she says. "We'll work something out."

"You're mad," I say.

I've had enough. I've decided that as soon as we are safely away I am going to call the police. Then I'm going to take the truck back to Eric. Then I will let the world do what it wants with me. I can't take any of this anymore.

But Carol makes me go with her to the cage. Together we heave it out of the water. As soon as it's on the shore I go inside and chase out the chicken. It flaps off towards the trees, stopping to scratch at something. I don't bother to go after it.

In a few hours, this place will be full of police helicopters and men with guns or poison darts and TV crews and RSPCA inspectors, but Carol insists we keep going, so I find the bag with the spanner and take off the side panels of the trap to make it easier to drag. We pull it behind some trees. It's not really hidden, but it's the best we can do.

Where's my dad?

Carol tells me it is only half-past six and that I might be able to get Eric's truck back to him without him even realizing it was gone.

"Then we can use it tonight," she says.

"But even if we catch him, what will we do with him?" I ask.

"He's not going to Birmingham," says Carol. "No way."

"But, Carol . . ."

She interrupts me.

"He's a saltwater crocodile, isn't he?"

"Yes, but they don't need saltwater to . . ."

"Well, then, we'll take him to the sea."

TWENTY

Eric is sitting on the wall outside his house waiting for me. I'm tempted to drive on but I'm stuck behind a milk truck. I really don't need a beating right now. I'm surprised he's up as it's still very early. I had hoped I'd get away with it and that I'd be able to "borrow" the truck again. No chance. I am too tired to think what to do, how to explain myself, how to save myself, so I just pull over onto the curb and switch off the engine.

Eric sits with his arms folded, looking at the ground.

"Out," he says.

I run my tongue over my teeth and climb out. I hand him the keys.

"Where's Dog?" he asks.

Dog. I'd forgotten all about him.

"He's fine," I say. "He's at the workshop."

"He'd better be," says Eric.

I square myself for the punch. I wonder if he'll go for the stomach or the head. I hope he's not going to fight dirty.

"I found your car," says Eric. "So I knew it was you."

He seems to be waiting for me to say something.

"Right," I say. I wish he'd hurry up. Once you've been beaten you can get over it. But the waiting is horrible. I hope he doesn't break my nose. I've never actually had a bone broken before either. I stand up on my toes to see if he's got a weapon hidden behind the wall.

But Eric seems unsure what to do. I think he is expecting an explanation and I realize he's shocked.

"Sorry," I mumble.

"Get lost," says Eric. He pushes me out of the way and gets in the truck. I watch him fire off down the street. I'm confused why he didn't hit me. I deserved it. I hope he hasn't got something worse planned for me. Maybe he has torched my car or something. I walk to the next road but the car is unharmed. Okay. If he's not going to hit me, why doesn't he call the cops? I look around expecting an ambush, but the street is quiet.

Verity gives me the dirtiest look ever when I come in. She's making a fry-up and the smell makes my mouth water.

"Where've you been?" she demands. "And why are you so filthy?"

"I've been out and about," I say. "Can I have some of that?"

She ignores me.

"Carol came in an hour ago. She's been out all night as well. What are you up to?"

So Carol hasn't told Verity. But for some reason I'm not as relieved as I ought to be.

"Just felt like some fresh air," I say. I notice three cardboard boxes lining the walls of the kitchen. My fishing rod is sticking out of one.

"What's this?"

Verity turns back to her frying pan. "You haven't been making much progress packing up your stuff, so I've done everything that's been lying around the place." She spoons hot oil over the eggs. "Don't worry — I haven't touched your room. But you need to get on with it, Stephen."

I'm tired. I have to sleep.

"Yeah, right," I say moving towards the stairs.

"Just a minute. Aren't you going to tell me where you've been?"

"Nope," I say. I lie on my bed. I can't sleep even though I'm knackered. Every single thing I do makes my life worse. And when I do finally doze off I dream of my dad.

Look, I'm not really worried about him. Disappearing is what he does best. If I had a heart attack each time he buggered off I'd have died before I could even walk. This is typical behavior. He's chickened out. That's the score. Believe it.

Later, I make myself have a shower.

I am drying myself off when there is a knock at the door. I wrap the towel round my waist.

"Come in."

It's Carol. She's bug-eyed with sleep.

"I didn't tell," she says, sitting on my bed.

"Why not?"

She smiles but doesn't answer.

I'm never going to be able to work this girl out. But I do know she is pretty twisted.

"So," she says, "what next?"

"Maybe we should give the police an anonymous tip-off," I say. "Before it's too late."

"Nah," says Carol. "They'll never believe you."

She's right. It's a crazy story.

We stare at each other for a few minutes and I get self-conscious about my bare chest.

"The cage is still there," she says. "We can try again."

Just then there is another knock.

"Stephen, telephone." Verity barges in. I am surprised because usually she waits until I say, "Come in." She looks pretty sick at seeing Carol on my bed.

"Telephone," she repeats, giving Carol a hard look.

Verity would hate worse than anything in the world for me and Carol to get together.

I pull on a T-shirt and go downstairs. For the first time in my life I am hoping that the person on the end of the phone is my father.

"Stephen, where's the ferret cage?"

Eric.

I am ordered into the workshop, and after I've eaten, I go. Look at me, trotting off to my slaughter like a little pig. I've got the feeling where you want to step out into the road so you get knocked over and break a leg or two so you don't have to worry about the next few hours. I'd quite like to be in a coma now. Maybe Eric will put me in one. But I don't think he will. He's had a good chance to hurt me and he hasn't. By now he will have found Dog, safe and sound, and that's got to help. He thinks I'm a mixed-up kid. All I was doing last night was behaving like one.

All the same I am pretty nervous when I enter the workshop.

"You look like shit," says Eric. He's heating up a bar of iron in his forge. The end glows hot orange. That would hurt. I lick my lips. I am thirsty but now is not the time to ask for a cup of tea.

"Why's my truck so dirty?" asks Eric. He pulls the bar out of the fire and places it on the anvil. He chooses a hammer and starts whacking.

He pauses for a breath.

"Where's the cage?"

He hammers some more then puts the bar back in the forge.

"And why did you bring my truck back?"

He turns to me.

"And why was this in my truck?"

It is a girl's pink hairslide. Carol's. I roll my eyes. The whole world thinks I'm a lady-killer.

I have a few choices at this point. I can make up something or I can tell the truth. Now, I'm not practiced at telling the truth and it makes me feel uncomfortable. But at the moment I am incapable of making up anything new. Dog runs in and licks my hand and I get this shot of warmth running up my arm. I don't want to be dragged off to the cops as a woman-murderer. As I start talking I feel like I am stepping off a cliff.

I tell Eric everything.

I start with the evening, maybe six or seven years ago, when my mum gets me out of bed because my dad's come home. I sit

160

in my pajamas on the sofa next to Selby. Selby's been out with his mates and has taken something or other because he's acting weird and he's snotting into his sleeve. I'm looking at my dad. It's been a while since I last saw him. He looks big. I remember that.

There's a massive fish tank on the floor in front of the telly, covered in a dirty white sheet.

"You have to keep him warm," says my dad. "Or he'll die."

Inside is this little lizard thing, floating about in manky water. It looks dead already. My mum looks like she's going to be sick.

"This is for you," says my dad. "Happy birthday, Stephen."

My birthday was three months earlier.

I tell Eric about how fast my birthday present grew, how he ended up in the bath, then how I smuggled him into my dad's lockup. I explained how I kept him alive, feeding him frozen mice from the pet shop and using a thermostat to check the water temperature. I'd told my family he'd died and that I'd buried him. Everyone believed me. There was some heavy stuff going on at the time and my mother wouldn't have noticed if I had a saber-toothed tiger in my bedroom. It's true. She went pretty mad and we all ended up moving in with Gran. It was my dad's fault. Whenever he came home, he'd be as nice as anything at first (giving me crocodiles, taking us to the pub, bringing home some chips for Mum). But after a few days he'd be plastered, and that's when we'd clear out to avoid a bashing.

Mum always got the worst of it.

What set him off that time was Victor. He lived across the road from us, and when Dad was in the nick, he'd come round sometimes to wire plugs and replace fuses. The sort of stuff me and Selby could have done but couldn't be arsed. He worked at the town offices doing something. He was all right. I never took much notice of him. But that time when Dad came back with My Little Present, Victor decided to show up with a sink plunger. (The kitchen sink was blocked.)

From the way Dad went on, it was like Victor had come round with an engagement ring. I'm not going into it. All I'll say is that Mum has shaved her head ever since.

I watch Eric. You know how sometimes you're telling someone something, and it's true, but it all sounds false? Well, the opposite is true now. Every detail I give makes my story sound more real. I show Eric the scar on my arm. I tell him about nicking chickens from the meat factory. Even so, he's having a hard time swallowing my story.

He raises his eyebrows when I tell him about the escape. But nods when I talk about how I encouraged him to build the ferret cage a certain way. I tell him about last night.

When I mention Carol, he interrupts.

"Hang on," he says. "So she actually saw it?"

I nod and keep talking. But I don't say I came away without my dad.

The forge has gone out and Eric has taken the phone off the hook. Dog is lying in the doorway, chewing on a bit of leather.

"There are a few problems with your story," says Eric. "One, why hasn't he attacked anyone yet, and two, how come the cold hasn't killed him?"

My mouth falls open. Maybe that's it. Maybe the lake is too cold and he's ill. That's why he didn't catch us last night. He's dying. Maybe if I just leave things as they are, he'll die naturally and one day someone will find a crocodile skull and wonder how the hell it got there.

"They need the sun to warm them up," says Eric. "I don't believe he'd survive an English winter."

I'd kept him warm when he was younger, but it hadn't occurred to me that the water cage would be too cold.

"He's managed somehow," I say.

I can tell Eric doesn't believe me, but he's fascinated all the same.

"Carol actually saw it?" he repeats.

"Ring her up," I say. "Ask her."

"So why don't you just go to the police?" asks Eric.

I give him a look.

"I can't," I say. "What if he's killed someone?"

TWENTY-ONE

I might as well sell tickets. I could open a mini zoo. It's funny to think that just a few weeks ago I was the only one who knew about my little pet. And now Eric and I are walking round the reservoir path, from the parking lot, to the pump cage. I wanted to sneak in via the pull-off, but Eric wasn't having any of it. He said he wasn't going to trespass on someone else's land. He said he's only come to collect the ferret cage and he's made me come with him. I walk on the right side of Eric, as far from the water as I can. I know my boy's in there. He has no reason to be onshore. There's no sunlight for him to bask in. He'll be lurking somewhere in the water, just below the surface, looking like a floating branch.

Eric obviously doesn't believe me. I'm surprised he's here at all, since he's got loads of orders to get through. I can't believe he just shut up the workshop in the middle of the day to come out here. Handy having your own business.

Eric snaps himself a stick from the hedge and swings it round, swatting at brambles and nettles.

From habit I look carefully around before leaving the path. But really it's a waste of time. My secret is out. Eric will either believe me or not. If he does, he'll tell the police; if not, he'll probably throw me in the lake. I might as well have a megaphone and start shouting:

I'M STEPHEN. I'VE ILLEGALLY KEPT A MAN-EATING CROCODILE AT THIS RESERVOIR FOR FOUR YEARS. I HAVE LET IT ESCAPE. IT WILL KILL YOU IF IT CAN. I'M HERE. HOLD ME RESPONSIBLE FOR THE DEATHS THAT ARE ABOUT TO HAPPEN.

I wonder how long I'll get. A couple of years? A few months? Community service? And at the end of it, I'll end up in the same place.

St. Mark's.

Just like my bloody dad.

I'm not that coldhearted, you know. I reckon he ran off the other night. I think this because if the crocodile got him, then why would he be trying to catch us all night? If he had nabbed my dad, he'd have eaten him right then or dragged him off somewhere for later. And there was no blood the next morning. The Internet says that crocs make a terrible mess of their victims, leaving bits of them everywhere. There was no carnage, was there? My dad is probably back at his hovel feeding cheap cat food to Malackie.

Yeah, right.

Eric gives me an odd look when I show him the ferret cage. Carol and I had piled bits of branches and bracken over it. The rope lies coiled just inside.

"You really did bring it up here," says Eric. He looks at the marks in the mud where we dragged it out of the water. Then he wants to see the pump cage.

"This is it?" Eric sounds surprised. He peers through the bars at the dark, scummy water.

"Yep."

"It stinks."

Eric walks slowly round the cage, pausing to poke the wobbly bars at the side. He's quiet.

"I'm not lying, Eric," I say. I can't stop twitching like a freak. I keep looking round at every crack, every snap. I keep a close eye on the shore.

"I almost believe you," says Eric. "But not quite."

Before I can stop him he has climbed into the cage through the bars and is standing on the concrete ledge.

"Don't," I say. "He might have come back. He can move really fast."

I'm worried. My boy thinks this place is home.

But Eric isn't bothered. He kicks a stick into the water and peers in.

"Come out, please." I can feel my scalp prickling.

"There's something over here." Eric starts edging round the narrow strip of concrete along the side. He yanks a mass of greenery, brambles, bracken, dead branches that cover the back wall into the water.

"Look, Stephen."

But I don't want to look. I don't want to see the twisting body leap up out of the water and grab him. I don't want to watch as the life is shaken out of him. I don't want this story to get any worse.

"For God's sake, Eric. I'm not joking." My voice cracks. Eric thinks this is a game. He has come up here not because he believes me but because he wants an afternoon off.

I think I see something dark in the water.

"Eric."

"There's a hole," he says. "Look."

I don't want to look. I can feel something horrible building up inside me. It makes me breathless and makes me want to stand very still. I never thought Eric was so crazy. He doesn't believe me and now he's about to lose his life.

I force myself to look. Eric is leaning right into the wall and I can't see his head.

"No way," he says.

This must be it.

"Eric." My voice sounds like a little kid's. "Get out."

"It's like a cave," he says. "Do you know about this?"

A cave? I don't want to get any closer. But I have to see what he is talking about.

I look at the water. There is no sign of the animal. But then I hear a splash.

"Eric."

The stupid bugger is moving stones and earth from the back wall and dropping them in the water.

"It's a burrow," says Eric, climbing through. "Come on."

"Eric."

I've got this funny feeling on the roof of my mouth. You know, like when you've eaten too much sugar and your skin goes numb and your spit goes globby? I force myself up to the bars. Eric has gone but I can hear something moving around.

"Eric?"

He doesn't reply and I feel panicky. God knows what he'll find in there.

I ought to go after him and make him come out. But that would be madness. I never imagined there was a hole in the wall back there. As my eyes get used to the light, I can see that it is just about big enough for a large crocodile to fit through.

The crocodile is probably still swimming around in the reservoir. Why would he break back into his cage? No, Eric is probably safe. I'm in more danger than Eric, out here, in the open. I might get pounced on and dragged into the reservoir.

I decide to wait just a little longer anyway.

"Stephen."

Eric's voice sounds like it's coming out through the hillside. He doesn't seem like he's in danger. So that means I can stay where I am, doesn't it?

"Come and look at this."

Even though his voice is muffled, I can hear surprise in his voice. I test the loose bars, look up at where they have come away from the cage. Even though the cage is old and rusty, the Beast must have had awesome strength to break out.

"Stephen." Eric sounds impatient. I peer into the water.

There is no motion, no sound, nothing. I think I'm safe. I think if he was in here, he would have gotten Eric by now.

I step over the bars and onto the ledge. How many times have I seen him lying on this ledge, motionless and with his jaws gaping open? I would never have imagined myself here.

"Stephen. It's fine. Come and look at this."

Eric's voice reassures me, and I manage to let go of the bar I am clinging to.

Hand over hand, I move round the edge. My arms are trembling and my knuckles are white. I want to look behind me and check the water but I am scared of losing my balance. The last thing I want to do is fall in. I'd die. I really would.

Eric is talking to me through the wall but I can't hear what he is saying. Finally I reach the back wall and I pull back the curtain of greenery. I'm hit by a draft of warm, stale air. As my eyes get used to the dark, I make out quite a large space. I yank at the ivy and brambles and pull them off into the water. I stick my head through the hole.

"Jesus."

Eric sounds so surprised I pull back and nearly fall back in the water.

Everything goes quiet. I stand very still and listen. I know what noises my boy makes. I know how he roars. I know the sound of his breathing. Sometimes he hisses, like a snake. Other times he lets out this noise, like he has a baby's rattle caught in the back of his throat. But I can't hear him now.

I think I might go back. So there's a cave behind the wall. So what?

Something moves behind the wall and I begin to step quickly back round the ledge.

A head thrusts through the hole.

"Are you coming or what?"

Eric looks at me.

"Wish I had a light," he says. "There's loads of stuff in there." I pass him my Maglite. He gives me a nod. "I'm beginning to believe you," he says.

It's a kind of animal burrow and it stinks of shit. Claw marks run over the walls. It's about the size of the inside of a minibus and it's pitch-black. Bones lie scattered here and there. Some are bigger than others. I don't look too closely. It is strangely warm, much warmer than outside. A massive iron girder reaches up from the floor to the ceiling.

Eric kicks it. "Could be something left over from the war," he says. "Or maybe this was an alternative site for the dam." He beckons for me to follow him to the back of the cave, and shadows leap over the walls.

"And this," he says, "is why I'm beginning to believe you."

He points the flashlight into a hole, about two feet across. Even in the poor light I can see it's deep. Eric proves it by kicking a clod of earth, which we don't hear land.

"Feel how much warmer the air is here?" he asks.

I nod. I can't speak.

"It's a borehole," he says. "Maybe the remains of a test pit or something, you know, for the dam. It's so deep we're getting warm thermals coming up from the ground. That's what's heating this cave." He shines the light into my face. "I admit I thought you were lying. But now I'm not sure."

I must be very stupid but I don't see why a hole in the ground makes Eric believe me.

"Reptiles need warmth to survive," says Eric. "They're cold-blooded. This cave is probably just warm enough to keep your crocodile alive during the winter." He kicks at a massive pile of rotting vegetation.

"And this is clever," he says. "Your croc has pulled this in from outside and used it to keep warm as it composts." He shakes his head. "I never knew they were so clever."

Neither did I. It freaks me out. Burrows, boreholes, compost.

My boy had all these things going on and I never knew about it. What else has he been up to?

This must be where he hid when the Dam Man was here. The walls are soft and damp. If my boy worked hard enough, he could have dug his way right out of the hillside.

"I want to get out of here," I say. Like I need to ask Eric for permission.

I scramble to the wall and climb through into daylight. I ease myself around the cage and clamber out over the broken bars. Logically I know I am in greater danger than in the cave but I am still massively relieved to be outside. Eric follows and we lean against the bars, not saying anything.

Eric dives into the bracken and pulls something out.

It is a shoe, or more accurately a boot. Boots, laces. They are pretty universal. A man's boot. New-looking, with brown leather. A yellow flash down the side. A stitched-on label saying Caterpillar.

My father's boot.

TWENTY-TWO

"There's no way," says Eric, "that we're setting it free in the sea. No way."

He turns into his yard and switches off the engine.

I shift in my seat. I hope Carol won't freak out. This is her master plan, after all.

"It's crazy," says Eric. "Apart from the risk to people, the water will be too cold. You'll kill it."

He doesn't have to convince me. I just want to get rid of it.

"We'll leave it somewhere safe," says Eric. He taps my arm. "Anonymously. At night."

I nod, feeling strangely high — maybe because I have all this unexpected help. I reckon Eric is enjoying himself. This is a big adventure for him. All the way home he was going on about how amazing it was. He likes a bit of danger, Eric. He likes to think he is a little bit of a bad boy.

He decides that we need a pig as bait. "Because that's what he's used to," says Eric. I wouldn't have thought of that. I think

Eric is going to be useful even though I still don't know that he really believes it.

Eric says he'll get the pig and call me later to arrange a time.

I drive myself home in my little Renault 5. Something wedged under the carpet catches my eye and I yank it out, nearly crashing into a yellow container at the side of the road.

It's a little bit of blue plastic. The stuff I used to wrap the pigs in. It seems like ages ago now. If I hadn't told my dad about him, none of this would have happened.

What about my dad? What about his boot? He probably lobbed the boot at the saltie. He loses stuff all the time. He lost a son; he lost a whole family, for God's sake. He's in a new pair of boots by now, nicked from somewhere. This is how he is. You should know this by now.

I'm approaching the turning to the Reynoldses' house when a figure steps off the verge and starts waving at me. It's Carol. What's she doing out here? It's started to drizzle and she hates getting wet. I slow and lean over to unlock the passenger door, but she shakes her head and indicates for me to wind down the window.

"What's wrong?" I ask.

She is pale and looks cold.

"Where've you been?" she demands suspiciously.

I kill the engine. This is going to take some explaining.

"I told Eric everything," I admit. "I had to."

"And is that where you've been? With Eric?" she asks.

"Yep, he's going to help us, only . . ." My voice trails off. I didn't want to tell her that Eric wasn't going to allow us to set it free in the sea.

"What?"

I think it over. "I think he doesn't know if I'm telling the truth or not," I say slowly. "I think he wants to believe me."

"But he still says he'll help?"

Carol mulls over this for a while.

"Look," I say. "Why don't you get in?"

"You can't come back," she says. "We've got to go."

"What?"

Carol keeps looking up and down the road as if she's expecting someone.

"So you swear you were with Eric all afternoon?" she asks.

"Yep," I say.

Carol picks her bag off the verge and crosses in front of my car and climbs in. I move to start up the engine but Carol puts her hand on the steering wheel.

"The police are here," she says.

"What?" I am so startled I push her hand off mine and almost crick my neck.

"They're waiting for you to get home."

I reel through my catalog of recent trouble. I really, really hope someone hasn't been killed by the croc. Or maybe Eric has decided to report me after all. Or maybe it's something to do with my dad. For a paranoid moment I wonder if there are closed-circuit TV cameras in the meat factory and they've seen me nicking the chickens. It could be anything.

I turn the ignition and the car fires into life. I begin a rapid three-point turn in the road, only it's so small it takes about eight points. But I'm not laughing. I decide to go back to Eric's. I can't risk getting arrested now, not when my luck is beginning to change. I've got Eric and Carol on my side now. This thing can be worked out; it doesn't have to end in disaster.

I am halfway to town before Carol speaks.

"Don't you want to know what's happened?"

I shrug. I can't focus on too many things at once. Like I said, they could pull me in for any number of things. Why dwell on it now?

"It's St. Mark's," says Carol.

I slow as we cross a railway line.

"What about it?"

"Somebody set fire to it this afternoon."

Won't any of this ever let up? I feel like a rock climber who finally reaches a ledge, then has it crumble under his fingers. We pass an old couple hobbling along, loaded down with shopping bags. For a second I envy them. What nice straightforward lives they must have; gardening and grandchildren, pensions and Mr. Kipling's Almond Slices. But then, who am I trying to kid? The old lady is probably deranged and her husband looks like an ex-con.

I take a different route to the workshop. I'm not going anywhere near St. Mark's. Do you blame me? I must have a revolving light on my head when it comes to arson. I'm like a beacon for the police. There must be tens of thousands of people living in this town. And it only takes one of them with a bottle of paraffin and a pack of matches to light a fire. So why blame me?

"What did Jimmy say?" I ask. Then I feel like kicking myself. Why should I care about what he thinks of me?

"He's shocked," says Carol. And she says something that

makes me feel mixed up. "He's worried about you. You've been missing for hours."

It's nice to be worried about, but Jimmy's only worried because he thinks I did it.

He thinks I might be trapped in the burning building.

"Someone told the police they saw you in the area," says Carol.

"I must be famous," I say.

I'm making jokes, but I'm bloody glad I've got Eric to give me an alibi.

Eric is surprised to see us back so soon. He looks pretty flustered. He says he's got loads of work to do before he finishes for the day. I hope he's not backing out.

"Let me just finish these," he says. He has a pile of railings to beat into shape with his hammer machine. He nods at Carol and tells us we can make ourselves a cup of tea in the office.

It's weird being back here. I mean, I don't expect Eric is going to give me that job now. I have a feeling he is just playing around. I'm worried he has a nasty surprise for me. Carol sits on the swivel chair and I perch on the desk, swinging my legs. Both of us sip black tea because the milk is lumpy.

I haven't got anything to say to her. For all I know she's going to spring something on me as well. I give her sneaky glances to see if I can work out what she's thinking but she's engrossed in an old newspaper she found in the trash. She warned me about the police. This is good. She is where I can keep an eye on her. This is also good. She knows about the crocodile. This is bad. But I know the truth about the village hall fire, and that is good. That will keep her down if she starts getting nasty.

She looks up from her paper and smiles. "Don't worry, Stephen — it's going to be all right."

I don't understand how she can be so calm. I don't understand how Eric can bang at a few bits of metal when all the time my boy is prowling around the reservoir.

A siren wails in the distance and I freeze. I want to crawl under the desk or jump out of the window but I can't. The noise fades but I can't relax. I listen to the steady thumping of the hammer machine. I imagine my head under the piston. It's how it feels these days. Only the machine is never switched off.

The door swings open and Eric comes in.

"You," he says, looking at me. "Out."

I jump to the floor and hurt my feet. They are cold. My circulation is bad and I landed too heavily.

"Wait in the yard," says Eric.

Of course I have to hear what they're saying so I shin up the brick wall, drop down into an empty yard of grassy tarmac, and creep up to the office window.

Unfortunately their voices are muffled but I manage to fill in the gaps. Eric is asking Carol if it's true. He's asking her if she's really seen it. I hold my breath. It would be just like Carol to lie now. Imagine that, if you will. I lean right into the wall. My head is only centimeters from the bottom of the window.

"I've seen it," says Carol.

There is a long silence. I wish I could see Eric's face. I'm sure he hasn't believed me up till now.

Eric swears and I feel a grin spread across my face.

TWENTY-THREE

Eric takes us to a greasy spoon round the corner. He orders a fry-up for himself, and me and Carol have a Coke. There are two blokes sitting at another table. I hope they're not undercover cops. They aren't talking to each other so we have to keep our voices down. I fiddle with the vinyl tablecloth and wish I had enough money for a triple bacon sandwich.

"Look," says Eric, "why don't we give the police an anonymous tip-off?"

"They'll kill it," says Carol. "With guns. You know they will."

Eric studies her, wondering what he's dealing with. In his book, shooting it would be no bad thing. Nor in mine.

"I thought you said he was going to help?" Carol turns on me.

"I feel like I'm on a reality TV show," says Eric. "Any minute they're going to jump out with the hidden cameras and call me a sucker."

"Then don't do anything," I say. "Just forget it, only . . ." I hesitate.

178

"Only what?" Eric's food arrives, and he plunges his fork into a runny yellow yolk.

"Can we borrow your truck, just for a night?" I look at my hands and bite my lip. This is almost funny. Selby always said I was a cheeky boy. He always said I had to push things just that little bit further. Why not? What have I got to lose?

Eric scoops up his egg and loads it into his mouth. I fiddle with the change in my pocket. I've got about a quid in there. I could afford a fried egg sandwich.

"You can come with us if you like," says Carol. "Just to keep an eye on your truck. You wouldn't have to do anything. Please say yes." She gives him one of her killer smiles.

Eric looks from one of us to the other. He swallows the last of his egg and sits back with a deep sigh.

"I may as well play along," he says. "After all, you only live once."

Food is amazing stuff. One minute you're walking along the street, feeling like shite, hardly able to walk straight and thinking you're going to pass out. Then you have a bite to eat and you're suddenly a master of the universe. Maybe Selby should have eaten more. Or maybe I'm just a freak, getting my kicks from food. But it's worked for Eric. Look at him!

I order an egg sandwich to take away and so Eric offers to buy Carol one but she says she's already had loads to eat today. But back at the workshop she helps me eat mine as we sit on the welding bench, watching Eric scurry around. He gets a tarpaulin and five wooden stakes and chucks them in the back. Then he makes me help him with this mechanical lifting arm. It screws into the truck. He says it works by hydraulics.

I'm glad he's coming with us. I'd never thought about how we were going to load the thing once we'd caught it. I guess I never really thought I'd get that far. I don't ask Eric what the stakes are for. I'm worried they're for something Carol won't like. Eric makes me get two planks from the yard and asks me to fetch the winch from his tool chest. The man has thought of everything. I don't really like him bossing me around, but I can't complain. All of this means he's taking me seriously.

It's late now, around half-past eight, so Carol phones home. She lies easily. I'm impressed. She makes up this story about staying at a mate's house.

"They don't believe me," she says, switching off her cell phone. "But we don't want them sending the police out after me, do we? They've left, by the way. Dad's got to call them when you get in."

The police. If we're not careful, they'll catch us before we've had the chance to do anything wrong. Maybe by now they've caught the person who did set fire to St. Mark's.

I hope so.

I have qualms about Carol. I can just about understand why Eric is helping me. He likes to think he operates outside the law. He sees this as a chance to stir things up a bit. He likes to be subversive. I think this is why he has me around. But what's in this for Carol? She could be out pulling blokes with her mates, all done up in her shimmery makeup, on her pink moped. Instead she's shivering in Eric's workshop, waiting to go and freeze her arse off all night, not to mention the danger she's putting herself in. She should be at home studying for her GCSEs, not hanging around a criminal like me and a freak like Eric. She sits asking Eric questions and flicking the chips of metal from the bench. She looks happy. Eric too is Mr. Lively himself, rushing about, grabbing a couple of old coats, an oil-stained blanket of Dog's, and a packet of cookies. It's only me who isn't saying anything. It's only me who's crapping himself. This is because when it goes wrong I know I will get the blame for all of it. And I still don't know where Eric is planning to take my boy. I don't want to ask him in front of Carol, because she still thinks we're taking him to the sea.

Eric couldn't get a pig so we stop at a supermarket. Eric gives Carol twenty quid and tells her to buy the biggest joints of meat she can find. She comes back with the most random selection ever. There are cheap sausages, a chicken, five pork chops, a leg of lamb, and three packets of bacon. Eric isn't impressed. He says it all looks too sterile and the crocodile will never smell it. He drives to the twenty-four-hour supermarket on the other side of town, losing us at least half an hour, where he goes in himself.

Carol and I wait in the truck, and I break open Eric's cookies.

We munch in silence, watching the late-night shoppers. It's Saturday night so there's lots of blokes buying pizza and beer. There's pissed-up students messing with the carts and quite a lot of couples with babies strapped to their chests. I wonder why all these people aren't doing something more interesting at ten o'clock on a Saturday night than going to the supermarket.

"How did he die?" asks Carol.

Crumbs get caught in my throat and I cough so hard my eyes water.

"Sorry," says Carol. "We don't have to talk about it."

Damn right, we don't. I recover from my fit and wipe my nose in my sleeve.

"I read everyone's file," says Carol. "I always have. Mum and Dad have got a filing cabinet in their bedroom."

I've seen it.

"They keep it locked, but I know where they hide the key. Whenever we get a new kid, I always sneak in and read their file. It's shocking what they don't tell me. But I like to know who's living with me. I like to know if I'm sleeping in the same house as a sex attacker or thief or a junkie or an abused kid. Wouldn't you?"

I nod. I'm not surprised. I'd do the same if I was her.

"So I read your file. I know about the cars and the school. I know your dad was violent. I know you lived with your gran for a bit when your mum got certified. But there's stuff missing. The social worker reports, the psychiatry assessments. It's like Social Services haven't told us everything about you." She takes the cookies from me and helps herself. "So naturally I worry."

"Mindy's pretty slack," I say. "She doesn't do any of the stuff she's supposed to."

"Yeah, right," says Carol. She sweeps crumbs off her lap as Eric staggers towards us in the orange lamplight, loaded with straining carrier bags.

There's a reason there's information missing. Years ago, when she was taking me somewhere, Mindy left my file lying on the car seat. When she got out to get petrol, I removed a load of papers. I've got stuff I don't want anyone to know. Like stuff about Selby. Like why I was put into foster care in the first place.

Mum was always a bit, I don't know, delicate. Selby says that when Dad got back from the Gulf War, she burned all his clothes because she thought they were poisonous. I can just imagine her doing that.

I wasn't dragged off into care by Mindy. Oh, no. It was Mum. It was Mum who went mad and said she couldn't cope. I thought we were fine, all of us living with Gran. But Mum asked Social Services for help. She said I was out of control.

She betrayed me.

It's a warm night. There's a bit of wind but it's mild and it's stopped drizzling. As Eric pulls open the loose wire in the reservoir fence, I notice the warm dampness in the air I'd smelled a few nights before. I'm glad winter is nearly over.

The water is gray with a strange shimmer. I don't go anywhere near it. I hear Eric talking to Carol clearly, even though they are standing some way off, fiddling with the cage. The trees lining the water are black. I worry that the water is too cold. That the Beast is not swimming and hunting but is stalking his prey aboveground. I have with me a metal poker from Eric's workshop. It has a sharpened point. It's heavy but I can't let go of it. I am listening for the smallest sound. It's like I can interpret any noise. That splash, that's a trout jumping. The crack in the distance is a cow rubbing itself against the fence. I will know the sound of the Beast. I will recognize the slide of his tail over the ground. I will hear his soft grunt. I know the sound of his breathing. I will sense him as soon as he comes anywhere near. He won't get a second chance. It's like I have two pairs of eyes and four ears. I am looking everywhere. My head feels like it's moving as fast as an insect. And I have another sense — I can feel when something is near. I don't know about death and God. But if there is any chance of it being real, then Selby is with me right now. He is encouraging me to keep breathing. He is looking into the darkness behind me.

We're not taking any chances. Once the trap has been set, the meat broken open and piled up, the rope attached and the whole thing pushed into the water, we all climb the tree. Carol and I make ourselves comfortable, sitting close to each other as before, only this time we have coats and blankets and food. Eric is reluctant and comes up last. He is in a funny kind of mood. He makes jokes but he seems pissed off with us.

"We should have brought a card game," he says. "How about Snap?"

He sits on the lowest branch. If the crocodile wanted him, Eric would be in easy reach. I tell Eric this but he says he'll be fine. I tell him he must whisper and he gives a kind of laugh but goes quiet all the same. After about half an hour he informs us he's going to check on the van and slithers down the tree. I watch him, my stomach feeling like a rock. I can't be responsible for his death. I am waiting to hear a soft hiss, waiting for Eric to scream, when Carol speaks.

"Robert made a real fuss about you leaving," she says. "He's really pissed off."

There's no noise from the water and Eric's footsteps have died away. The animals and birds are silent.

"He died from sniffing glue," I say. "Selby," I add quickly, in case she didn't realize.

I feel her tense up.

"Stupid bugger," I go on. "He'd stopped doing it ages ago. He was seventeen, for Christ's sake. He had more dignified ways of getting a buzz. But he was found dead in the parking lot by the swimming pool. The glue had dried over his nose and around his mouth and he still had the bag in his hand. At first no one believed that was what killed him. Kids are doing it all the time and it's rare for anything to go wrong like that. Usually it's because they've fallen under a car or something, not because of the glue itself."

I keep talking. I've never said this to anyone before. I tell her that after Selby died my mum got ill again. She got so bad she wouldn't even have us at Christmas anymore.

I don't tell Carol that Selby was also surrounded by cans of lighter fuel. I don't say that he had vomit all over his coat and face. I don't say he was lying in a puddle of his own piss. I don't say that the paramedic had to find a handkerchief to put over Selby's mouth and nose before he started the mouth-to-mouth because as he said to his mate in a voice he hoped wouldn't be heard, that he was going to be sick and this lad was just scum anyway.

I don't tell Carol this because she might ask me how I know.

*   *   *

185

As it gets later, Eric moves farther up the tree, a branch for every hour. Even though he is still skeptical about all of this, it's easy to let your imagination go mad out here. It's such a dark night. The clouds are covering the moon and the stars. Of course our eyes have become accustomed to the darkness, but it's difficult to tell what anything really is.

My imagination isn't going mad. I know there's a twelve-foot reptile nearby, unless he's gone. I read they can travel overland to new water sources. But I don't think he would. This is where he is used to being fed.

I still have this small hope that the cold has killed him. Maybe you think I'm mean. It's not the crocodile's fault it was smuggled into this country. It should be in some Indian river with its own kind. And I eat meat, so why shouldn't it do likewise? But you know I've looked after this thing for years. You know how I've spent all my money on meat and made up hundreds of lies to cover its tracks. And what thanks do I get? The bloody thing only tried to eat me! If it were dead I could finally relax. I had the right idea in the first place. I should have got hold of a gun some-how and shot it. Look at me — I've got a truck, a girl, and a blacksmith. I've got a cage and a pile of supermarket meat. I've got a hydraulic arm and a thirty-foot rope. If I've managed to get these things, why didn't I get a gun?

Carol's not asleep. I can tell by her breathing. She hasn't spoken since I told her about Selby. She can go home and get out her word processor and type out my missing notes now. She can pop them in my file. The tree trunk is biting into my side. I move to make myself more comfortable. I wonder how many days we can keep this up. Now that the police are after me it has to be in the next few days. I wonder if Jimmy will turn me in if I go back

186

to get some fresh clothes. And I could do with a bath. I look up at Eric. He's above us now, clinging to his branch. Would he put me up for a few days while we catch it?

You know, I could get out of this tree right now. I could some-how get back to town, get my car, and drive, I don't know where. Maybe up north. I could make a new start in a new place where the police aren't looking for me. St. Mark's isn't waiting for me anymore, so I've got nowhere to go. Correction. I've got every-where to go.

My arse cheek has gone numb. I shift over and Carol com-plains that I am squashing her.

"This is crazy," whispers Eric. "What am I doing here?"

I don't think he wants an answer.

"How's Terry?" I ask Carol quietly.

"I have no idea," she says.

We sink back into silence.

My boy has got to be hungry, hasn't he? Surely he can sniff the meat. I think even I can smell it from here. What's the matter with him? Maybe he really is dead.

The wind is getting up. Small waves lap round the trap. I realize that despite my coat, the blanket, and Carol, I'm getting cold. It starts in my feet and hands and the tips of my ears and gradually spreads over my body. A support worker took a group of us up to the Millennium Dome when I was a kid. I don't know what all the fuss was about. I thought it was cool. I especially liked the machine that you walked through and it reflected your body. The hottest parts of you were red and the coldest were blue. I got embarrassed because according to the machine, the hottest part of me was my crotch. Mind you, I was only about twelve or thirteen and I was pretty obsessed with sex at that age. If I was standing in front of that machine now I reckon all of me would be a pale blue.

Something has changed. I can feel it. The others know it too even though nobody is saying anything. It's as if all of us have been dragged up from our thoughts back here to this tree, this lake, this cage.

A tiny sound comes out of Eric, and I look at the shore.

Something dark is moving out of the water.

An animal crawls and slips over the mud on all fours towards the cage.

TWENTY-FOUR

There is a small pain in my arm, and I realize Carol is pinching me. I brush away her hand and slowly, slowly untie the rope round the trunk that holds the cage open. I don't take my eyes from the shore.

Eric is swearing under his breath.

I need to keep the rope at the right tension or the door will move and my boy will get scared off. But I need to be ready to let the door fall before he gets away.

Eric has put some clips on the lower bar so that when the door shuts, it is held in place.

It might be the bad light, but I could swear the crocodile is tired. He moves slowly and cautiously and seems to be dragging his legs. Carol has my arm again. I can't breathe. I know something is going to go wrong. He will suspect us and swim off. Or he'll smell me and come hunting for fresh meat. There is a cough building in my throat but I keep it down and my eyes stream.

The crocodile stops at the mouth of the trap. We hear his

breathing as he smells the night air. He knows there's meat inside.

Go on, my son.

He's hungry and cold. He needs the food to survive.

There is a loud rattling noise and he lunges forward. Hardly knowing what I am doing, I yank on the rope and the door slams shut. I scramble out of the tree, half falling to the ground, and run towards the cage.

"Stephen, wait," Eric shouts at me, but I ignore him. Have I got him? Have I? Have I caught him, Selby? Of course I have. I must have. I slip over the mud and come to a sudden halt.

He thrashes against the sides of the cage, roaring and fighting. I step back. His body seems to bounce off the metal panels, making them shake. I don't see how they can possibly contain him. He smashes into one side, then the other. Then I see something that turns me cold.

His tail is still sticking out the end of the trap.

The door has not closed properly. If he backed out at the right angle he could escape.

I don't know what I am doing now, but it feels like jumping off a bridge. I get this mad surge of energy and I run to the cage.

"Here I am!" I shout. "Come and eat me."

The animal rushes forward and his snout crashes into the end of the cage and for an instant his tail sweeps inside. I sprint to the back. I slam down the door and jam it against the bars. I hear a double click. He's trapped.

He's mad now, smacking himself around, his massive jaws gnawing at the bars, trying to get a grip. Every bit of his energy has returned. I step away from the cage and watch. I want to run but I can't. My brain is telling me there is no need, but my body wants me back up that tree, or in Eric's truck and driving fast.

The clouds have cleared now and I can see him better. He stops struggling and eyes me, panting and clawing one webbed foot into the floor of the cage. His long lower tooth juts from his jaw. I can't take my eyes off him. I am face-to-face with my worst nightmare.

"Get back," shouts Eric from a long way away.

The crocodile stops panting and goes as still as stone. We watch each other. He's like something dead and fossilized, he's so still. He could be a pile of rocks. Only a small area under his chin pulses up and down, letting me know he's still thinking of me.

I don't know how long we're like this, caught up in each other's eyes. Listen to me, I sound like I'm in love with the thing. But I'm not. I hate him. At least I think I do. It's getting lighter and I can see more of the markings on him, the gray-black spots and the thick ridges on his skin. And I can smell him too. He smells of dirty water and blood.

I hear footsteps. Eric comes first, followed by Carol. In the morning light I can see the expression on Eric's face. He is wide-eyed like a kid on an E. Carol hangs back. She looks ready to run.

"Has the latch worked?" Eric asks softly. I nod, and we all jump back when the animal lets out a massive breath, sounding like the garbage truck when it pulls up outside your house.

We all look at it for a long time, gradually edging closer.

"It's huge," says Eric. As we stand there, a flock of geese fly overhead and I notice the crocodile's eyes flicker. He hasn't touched any of his meat. He's scattered it around the trap. He has a pork chop on his shoulder and his front claws rest in a mound of sausages.

This ought to be funny, but it isn't.

Eric's watch beeps the hour and it's like we all wake up.

"Five o'clock," says Eric. "Move."

I am weak now. I can only take orders, and though I carry the logs to the shore and fetch the winch from the truck and attach one end to the tree, it is Eric who ties the rope to the trap and lays the logs in a line in front of the cage. He gives me the signal to start working the winch. He made that cage himself so he knows how strong it is. But I know how powerful my boy is and I am wary. He's quiet now, even when he is winched up onto the logs. He scrabbles with his legs but there is no major movement.

When I've watched crocodiles being caught on telly, they tie up the jaws. I suggest this to Eric and he tells me to go ahead because he's not stopping me.

The cage edges forward, rolling on the logs. It is my job to keep winching and Eric's job to replace the logs ahead of the cage, one by one as they are rolled over. It's slow work and I get hot. I worry that what we are trying to do is impossible.

We are pulling him up off the shore and on the grass when he starts hissing.

"Watch it," I call. "He's building up to something."

"Keep going," Eric shouts through his teeth. He is breathing louder than the crocodile as he pushes and shoves. Carol has obviously decided that being a girl has its advantages and is staying well clear. I thought she had more guts than this, but I can't really blame her. This is my problem, not hers.

Then the crocodile starts bellowing and I am so surprised I let out this noise, like a girl's scream. In any other circumstances it would be embarrassing. He grips the mesh at the front of the cage and tries to turn himself over. He's trying to do his death roll.

"Get out of the way," I shout, but Eric is already backing off. The tail lashes round the cage, slamming into the bars. The noise echoes across the water. It's so loud I expect the warden to turn up at any minute.

The cage rocks as the crocodile slams into the mesh. I back off fast, hoping to hell the door clips will hold. There is a thud as the cage tips off the logs and onto the grass. For a couple of seconds the crocodile is upside down, and I look at its pale belly. If I had a knife or a spear, that's where I'd stab it. The fall seems to have knocked the breath out of it and it goes still again. Eric shouts at me to help him move the cage back onto the logs but my feet won't move.

"Stephen, come on. It'll be light soon."

He's bloody mad. I don't understand how he can't see the power of the thing. How can he stand to get so close?

Carol slides down the mud to help and together they wedge the logs under the cage and signal for me to start winching again.

Mud and exhaustion. Heavy breathing. Pushing, pulling, straining with every bit of strength in my arms and legs. Slipping over once, twice, then cutting my lip on a stone. Blood in my mouth. Carol taking my place at the winch, me pushing the cage from the back, checking the clips. It's getting lighter. Fear that someone will find us. Move the winch to a farther tree. Move the crocodile past his old pump cage. He hates moving; he is calmer when we have a rest. Jump clear as he starts rolling again. Move back in when he stops. Pulling him and rolling him up through the trees to the fence. Watching the meat smear over his body and roll against the mesh. Pink mud beneath him. Winching him right up to the truck. Carol touching my arm. She takes off and goes to sit in the truck. She's not going to help anymore. Nobody's saying anything except Eric, who shouts instructions. A feeling of relief even though it is now nearly six o'clock and we can hear cars on the road.

Eric leans into the side of his truck. I can smell his sweat. He has taken off his sweater and shirt and is working bare-chested. I find this strange. I want as much between me and those teeth as I can get.

I lean towards Eric. "Where are we taking him?" I speak in a low voice, though Carol has the windows wound up.

"St. Matthew's," says Eric, unclipping the sides of the flat-bed. "In Bexton."

I must look surprised.

"Good road access, massive graveyard, no security cameras, unlikely to be populated first thing in the morning." Eric wipes the sweat from his face with his arm. "And I expect the first person to find him is either going to be a grave digger or the vicar."

Eric attaches a hook to either end of the cage. "And if he does get out of the cage, I know the railings are good and strong." He clips on the chains. "Because I made them myself."

Eric operates the mechanical arm. The chains creak and something metal screeches. The machine makes a humming noise that's too loud for the early morning quiet.

The cage wobbles and leaves the ground. I hope he doesn't kick off now. I hold my breath as it climbs higher.

The cage swings in the air and I have to guide it with my

hands. For a few minutes I have a live crocodile swinging over my head. I will not forget it. I am constantly stepping away from his jaws. I only touch the cage where his tail is rammed against it. I don't want him to see me. I can see his underside clearly and his webbed feet and claws. The plates in his tail get smaller and smaller towards the tip, in a perfect pattern, each plate interlinking with the next. I get a strange feeling that everything is going to be all right. In just a few hours this thing will have gone out of my life forever.

"Stephen, for God's sake," calls Eric. He is annoyed that I've been standing still, just looking at the gently swaying body above me. As the crane swings round towards the truck, I put my hand on the bar and accidentally touch his side. The skin is hard and cold. He doesn't feel alive. I trace his armor with my finger. I can't believe he hasn't eaten me yet. I feel weak and soft. I would tear so easily. He'd kill me in seconds. I hear ringing in my ears. I take my hand away almost reluctantly. I guide him onto the truck and he lands with a clunk and the whole truck shudders.

My fingertips are burning hot.

We drive up through the field of cows, the wheels spinning and spitting out mud. The cows stand well clear of us, but each one is watching. They know.

Eric is driving too fast. He keeps saying how late it is and how we'll never reach the graveyard in time. He wants us to be gone by seven. We pass the Reynoldses' house and Eric asks Carol if she wants to get out. I think we are both worried about her because she is so quiet. She looks at him as if he is mad even though her clothes are wet and muddy and her teeth are chattering. I want to put my arm around her. It wouldn't be difficult; we're all cramped together in the front seat. But I don't know how she'll react. I give her Eric's coat to put over her legs. She doesn't mind that, so I grab her hand and squeeze it.

I don't let go.

As we approach town, Eric pulls over onto a side road.

"We're not taking it to the sea, are we?" says Carol when Eric is outside, checking the tarpaulin is secure.

"The sea's too cold," I say. "It'll kill him."

"He's done all right so far," Carol points out. "He'd be better off free."

"But he wouldn't just swim out to sea," I say. "He'd hang around the coast and eat people."

Carol puts her forehead on the window and breathes out sharply. I recognize the noise. It means she's annoyed. I get an inkling of worry. I hope she's not going to start being Carol-ish. Now is definitely not the time. I scrabble in the glove compartment and find the remains of the cookies and offer one to her. She takes it and crunches hard. I hope the sugar works on her.

Eric stands at the door. His face is muddy and tired-looking and his T-shirt is covered in mud.

"It's no good," he says. "We'll have to hide it in the workshop today and dump him at the graveyard tonight."

I shake my head. There's no way it will happen like that. The crocodile will make a noise, or die, or escape, or someone will come into the workshop. Besides, I've got the police looking for me and I can't do anything about it until I've gotten rid of him. I don't need any more trouble. The police are bound to come to

Eric's workshop and ask questions, then the whole lot of us will be in big trouble.

But Eric is determined. "It's too late for today," he repeats. I say that if the Beast escapes, they'll shoot him. But Eric has made up his mind. He asks me to pass him some spring ties and I find them under my seat. He goes around to the back of the truck.

Now you know me well enough to know that I sometimes get these crazy urges. It's like I am in a little rubber dinghy and I'm being pulled out to sea by the tide and there is nothing I can do about it.

Uh-oh, I think as I recognize that familiar feeling. I've got this massive rush. Something is going to happen.

Quickly I slide across into the driver's seat and turn the ignition key.

Carol looks up in surprise, then grins.

"Hey!" shouts Eric.

I push it into first and do a U-ey in the road.

"To the sea, to the sea," screams Carol, and I floor the accelerator. In the rearview mirror Eric holds out his hands in disbelief. He gets smaller and smaller.

He should have learned never to trust a thief.

TWENTY-FIVE

It's half-past six in the morning and we're driving too fast. The adrenaline is fading and I realize I don't want to draw attention to myself. I slow down.

"It's forty minutes to Salcombe sands," Carol says happily.

She's dreaming. I'm not going to let this thing free in the sea. I'll never be rid of it. It will eat someone and then their dad or brother will come looking for me with a knife. Or it will find its way back across country to the reservoir and lie in wait for me. No, I've got more definite plans.

There's an old quarry close to the meat factory. The bottom is full of water and in summer all the kids swim there and the lads dare each other to jump off the highest ledge. I've never jumped. I don't like deep water. Do you blame me?

I remember there is a long, sandy road of about four miles leading to it and a sheer drop before the road winds down to the water.

That's right, a sheer drop.

Crocodiles need to breathe. If, for example, one was dropped from a great height, in a cage, into a deep lake, it would drown even if it survived the fall. And he'd probably die of the cold before he drowned. So I'm offering him three ways to die.

He would sit looking like a pile of stone in an old cage at the bottom of a deep lake. I reckon a dead crocodile looks pretty much like a live one; all that hard skin must take some breaking down. It will be so still and quiet down there, he'd sit like that forever, back in fossil land where he belongs.

Yes, of course I'll go through with it.

I turn off the main road and start up towards the quarry. We drive past the meat factory entrance. Thank God I'm not going back there again.

"Is this a shortcut?" asks Carol.

I don't say anything and she grunts and curls up in her seat, her knees against the dashboard.

A few miles from the quarry I notice a red light is on. It's the petrol light. How long has it been like that? We haven't got enough petrol to get to the quarry. Bloody Eric, why can't he be more organized?

Carol notices me looking at the light.

"Ah," she says.

I stop the truck and get out, taking the keys with me just in case Carol is as mad as I am. Eric may carry spare petrol in his truck, but I'll have to look for it.

There is no noise coming from the back. I decide this is a good thing and I lift a corner of the tarpaulin. Oh, God! There he is. Staring right at me. He has me fixed in his eyes. I imagine I can see my reflection in his pupils. He knows what I am going to do with him. His throat is moving up and down really quickly. If I didn't know better, I'd say he was frightened, but we've all heard of crocodile tears, have we not? There is more blood on him than there ought to be. I see a gash down the side of the body. It's oozing red. He breathes out and I get a waft of his stale, warm breath. How did he get hurt? It must have been when he rolled the cage over, or maybe it happened before and it was too dark for us to see. Whatever it was must have been pretty sharp to puncture that skin.

There is no petrol in the back. But if I can find another car I can borrow some petrol from it.

Cars out here? I'm out of my mind; there are only cooking-oil farmers and red-diesel tractors. No, the only place I'm likely to find a nice petrol vehicle I can tap is at the meat factory.

I look at my watch. It is ten to seven. The first workers will arrive in forty minutes. I don't know if I have enough time but I have to do something. I start up the truck and reverse back down the road. Carol is talking to me but I don't hear what she is saying.

The meat factory parking lot is deserted except for a solitary vehicle. It's a Ford Fiesta and it's very clean, inside and out. From this intelligence and the fact that it's so early, I decide that it's the cleaner's car. I am about to set to work when there is a hiss from the back of the truck. I have an idea.

Throwing him in the quarry isn't an option anymore. I'm out of time. I'm going to abandon him in the meat factory parking lot. It's as good a place as any. Someone might even give him a chicken.

My boy is going to die. He has an evil wound in his side. He is bleeding to death. He's a condemned man. I, on the other hand, have nothing wrong with me. I just need to get rid of him and get away before I get in even more trouble.

The gray walls of the factory loom over us. A door has been

left open. That must be the cleaner. I hope she is too busy with her newspaper to look out at the parking lot. In just over half an hour the drones will be arriving and I am going to give them all a day off. I knew I'd be running the place one day. I'm getting a bit of a kick out of this. Imagine Naomi's face! I wish I could see it, but I'll be long gone by then.

I strip off the tarp and the crocodile gives this massive shiver. I hope he doesn't die yet. It would be less fun for them all to find a dead crocodile in the parking lot. A live one will be much more interesting.

I knock at the truck door.

"Come on," I say to Carol. "I need your help."

She is sulking and won't look at me.

"What's going on?"

"He's hurt," I say. "The sooner someone official finds him, the better." I watch her face carefully. I don't want her getting upset now. "If we leave him here, they'll call a vet, who'll tranquilize him and sort him out."

Obviously I have no idea if this is true.

"But we're taking him to the sea."

I admit I nearly give way then, she looks so sweet and sad. And so unlike Carol.

"It's too late for that now."

I think she sees we have no other choice.

"Carol." I haul open the door. "Please."

"All right, all right." She climbs stiffly out of the truck and yawns. "How is he?"

"Come and help me work the crane," I say. I want her to work it while I guide the cage. I don't want her too close to his jaws. If anyone is going to lose a hand it should be me.

I unscrew the control panel and look at the knobs. It looks simple enough. I've never driven a digger but it reminds me of those arms you get in the arcades, where you put a quid in and never win the cheap watch. I practice moving the gears without the chains on and when I've got a rough idea I get Carol to come and look. Then I fix the chains to his cage. I have to stretch right out over him to do it. He is very still and I work quickly.

"Up," I say. The chains lift and go taut and the cage moves off the truck.

The cage goes higher and higher until I tell Carol to swing it round and away from the truck. She moves it the wrong way and a corner catches on the cab. He is hissing now. I know what this means. He is going to kick off again. But the hissing dies away. Carol swings it back. There's a new dent in Eric's truck.

"Down," I say. The cage comes crashing down. "Slower!" I shout, but she can't hear me. It comes down as fast as falling and hammers into the concrete with a loud clang.

"Sorry," says Carol.

I think he is winded or something because he doesn't move but lets out this horrible squeaky noise. At the same time I feel this massive pain in my side, like I'm the one who's been hurt. Then the pain goes away. I think we've injured him really badly this time. But I haven't got time to see if he's all right. I've got to get us away.

I fetch Eric's tool kit and a half-full bottle of lemonade and run over to the Fiesta.

I empty the drink on the ground and fish around for a suitable tool. I find a hammer and chisel. Carol looks confused so I tell her to get in the truck where it's safe.

Look, I'm not a good boy, okay? But I haven't cut any fuel pipes for years. I didn't think I would be doing it again but I'm bloody grateful I learned how. It's one of the sneakiest types of car crime. You come back to your vehicle and can't work out why it won't start. *Sorry about that*, I say to the car. I feel calm. It's nice to be doing something I actually know about for a change.

I'm lying under the car when I hear the banging and I nearly knock my head off as I sit up. The cage is rocking. He has the mesh in his teeth. He's going to roll. I sit there with petrol pouring out over my jeans and I can't move. He's mad now. He lets out this bellow, then another one. He sounds horrible, like a lion. But the roar is deeper than that; it's like the lowest, meanest sound I've ever heard. His tail thumps against the cage and it tips right over. He scrabbles around, getting upright, getting a new grip. I check to see that Carol is still in the truck, and I see her face pressed against the window at the back, looking down on him. I'm glad I took those keys out. If I was her, I'd drive off now.

He pushes back and the door clangs open. I can't believe it. The clips must have come undone when we dropped him. He doesn't know it's open yet; he's still beating at the sides. The cage turns again and again, rolling towards me.

It is just a matter of time before he gets out but I can't move. I'm frozen, like in a nightmare. Everything is happening so quickly I can't get a grip on it. All I can do is watch. Somehow he manages to tip the cage right up on its end. He's nowhere near death yet. He's more powerful than ever. The cage crashes to the ground.

He isn't in it anymore.

I'm silent as I watch him run towards me, his mouth wide

open, showing me his thick yellow teeth and bloody mouth. I wish I was the sort of person to pass out, but I'm not. You know that.

"Selby," I say as he rushes at me, knocking me flat on the ground. I'm being pulled over the tarmac, but I can't feel anything.

There is a gray sky. Out of the corner of my eye I see the lemonade bottle half full of petrol. Enough to start a fire, enough to scare him off. But I haven't got the time. It's all over.

I'm not moving anymore. I wonder where he's going to bite me first. My head is the obvious choice; he could twist it off in seconds. Or maybe an arm. He's been dying to eat me for years, ever since he tasted my blood all those years ago when I moved him from the lockup to the reservoir. It must have driven him crazy, having me so close, when he knew exactly how I tasted, how warm and rich my blood is. Close to the stuff of his dreams but unable to have it.

The taste of paradise.

I don't know why I think that. I think I'm trying to make my death easier. It's nice that I'm going to make someone happy at last.

"Stephen!" Carol screams.

I don't think she'd taste good. She's too skinny and mean.

"Stephen, look."

She wants me to look, Selby. She wants me to look when I'm about to die. What does she want me to see? A hot-air balloon? A flock of geese? A crazy man in a microlight? Nothing is important enough for me to look, nothing. The woman is off her mind. She's not the girl for me, you know. She's mental.

Something grabs my arm and I wait patiently for it to rip off.

I imagine my head banging on the tarmac as I am rolled over. *BANG BANG BANG.* It's quite funny, really. I will look like a piss head falling down the stairs. How am I doing? I'll see you soon anyway. You can tell me face-to-face. That is, if I have a face left. I'm quite good at this death thing. Maybe it wasn't so bad for you after all.

"Stephen. Look."

It's Carol. I can't have died, because she's definitely not an angel.

I sit up.

He's running down the slope to the meat factory. His tail slips through the scrubby low hedge. He moves easily across the concrete. He knows exactly where he is going. I bet he can smell the meat. I bet it's driving him crazy. There's nothing wrong with him now. He effortlessly climbs the few steps to the open door and slides inside.

TWENTY-SIX

I stare at the factory wall. I can't breathe. Then I get this rush of air in my chest and I let out this explosion. It's half a laugh and half a scream. I sound like an animal. I've definitely lost it now. Weird noises keep coming out. It's like my brain has lost control of my vocal cords. Carol is all pale like she's about to pass out.

I finally manage to speak English.

"Let's go."

I grab the bottle of petrol and try to open the fuel cap on the truck. Like my mouth, my fingers won't work properly and I drop the keys. The second time I drop them, Carol picks them up and unlocks the cap for me. She unscrews the lid, takes the bottle, and feeds it in. A lot of petrol comes right back out again and splashes on the wing.

"Stephen," says Carol. She's examining the back of my jacket. I twist around to look. There's a long rip in the fabric.

"Whoa," I say. "Check my back." I lift up my jacket and top and feel Carol's fingers run over my skin. I wouldn't be surprised if I was badly hurt. I probably can't feel the pain because of the adrenaline.

"It's okay," says Carol. "There's nothing."

I pull back my clothes and grab Carol's hand. I just need to hold it for a few seconds. I think I might be sick.

"We have to go," she says.

We get in the truck, and I manage to turn and we burn off up the drive. As I steer out of the meat factory turning, my head clears a bit and I no longer have the retching feeling.

He dragged me along the parking lot with his teeth. And he let me go.

Why?

"Concentrate," snaps Carol as we hit a bend too fast and swerve over the road.

We are bombing along the lane towards the main road when we pass the minibus full of my factory pals. The driver stares but I don't think any of them recognize me. They're all too busy trying to stay awake.

"Oh, God," says Carol.

She's right. This is definitely the time to be talking to the man in charge.

Ten minutes later we're heading to town on the main road when a police car flashes past, sirens howling, then another. I imagine the cleaner trying to convince the coppers to come.

Police, please, there's a crocodile rampaging round Marshall's Meat Factory. Can you come quickly — he's eating my leg? Thanks.

Promote the man, I say. He must have amazing powers of persuasion. Still, I hope he's all right.

"Pull over," orders Carol, because just ahead is Eric with his thumb sticking out. I'm not surprised he hasn't managed to get a lift. He looks like my dad. A rough old tramp.

I don't know if I should stop. What if Eric kicks us out? But Carol insists, so I slow down and get a blast on the horn from the Audi behind.

Eric recognizes the sound of the engine and turns to face us. He's not happy. He looks like he's trying not to cry. I reckon I've got a fifty-fifty chance of a beating. What do you think? He had every excuse to do it last time I nicked his truck but he didn't. But I've gone and done it again so he might think I need a proper lesson rather than the guilt trip he laid on me last time. But I'm not scared. I'd rather have Eric do me over than a crocodile. At first Eric says nothing, he just gestures for me to move aside. I'd quite like to get out and get in the other door so Carol is between us but I don't want him driving off and leaving me here with all these pigs about.

"Where is he?" he asks.

I can't speak so Carol answers.

"We ran out of petrol, so we left him at the meat factory."

"Anyone see you?"

"No," says Carol.

Eric grunts and takes off. He's driving too fast, crashing the gears and overtaking the wrong cars.

We drive for some time with nobody saying anything. No less than seven police cars and two riot vans pass us. And as we get near town an RSPCA van burns by.

"You two are nasty little shits," says Eric.

I can't protest, because it's true.

Back at the workshop we stand around awkwardly. Dog acts

really weird. He won't come to any of us. I reckon he can smell the croc.

"I've done so much for you," says Eric. He's fiddling with his radio to see if he can find anything on the news.

"I know," I say. "I'm sorry."

Eric puts down the radio and gives me a sickened look.

"You're not really sorry, are you, Stephen?"

"No," I say. But in a way, I am.

Carol comes back from the bog. She's washed her face and retied her hair. Women are crazy. They'd want to look their best if they were going out to face a nuclear winter.

"Have you told him?" she asks.

"Told me what?" Eric takes a long drink of water from his bottle.

I kneel and scrape a chunk of mud from my shoe. I pick it up and deposit it in the bin. If Carol can keep it together, so can I.

"He escaped," I say. "The door broke open."

Eric goes pale.

I tell him we saw it run into the meat factory.

Eric collapses on his welding bench.

"Thank God it didn't happen here," he says. He sees the rip in my jacket. "How did that happen?"

I swallow. I can't speak.

"It had Stephen in its mouth," says Carol. "Just for a few seconds."

Now I do feel weak. I join Eric on the welding bench. No one says anything for ages. We sit and listen to the morning traffic. Every other vehicle seems to have a siren.

Then, to my amazement, Eric pats my arm and nods at Carol.

"Take her home."

Of course I can't stay away. After dropping Carol off, I park my Renault in a field near the meat factory, making sure it can't be seen from the road. Then I skirt along the hedges to the boundary surrounding the parking lot. I have to duck into the hedge three times as a police helicopter flies over. I find myself a nice little spot in a thick bush where it's not too damp and there's a good view of the parking lot.

It's pandemonium. There are police everywhere. There are megaphones and guns and two RSPCA vans. There's a helicopter and a TV crew and a couple of blokes in white paper suits hanging round the doorway. A black van arrives and ten cops in riot gear get out.

They've cordoned off part of the factory with red tape, and police are trying to get people to stay back but everyone is really curious. It's like a siege or something. I recognize Naomi in the crowd. She doesn't look sleepy now. A couple of the butchers stand close together. They don't look so big outside. Maybe it's because they're not holding their knives. I can't take my eyes off the door. It's closed, and three armed police are guarding it. They don't know whether to look at the door or at the crowd. I wouldn't want to turn my back on that door, I can tell you.

A woman is helped out of the back of an ambulance. She's leaning heavily on the paramedic's arm. I suppose she must be the cleaner. Poor old biddy. The crowd cheers. She's given a folding chair and cup of something.

Then everyone falls silent to listen.

He's roaring. The sound echoes out over the parking lot and

everyone moves back. Some people even get into their cars. He's still alive, then. I don't know why, but I feel pleased. To be honest, I feel sorry for the poor animal. I hope they don't kill him. None of this is his fault. I only hope he's had a great time in there. I imagine him tearing the cow carcasses down from their hooks, hoovering up chickens, and munching kebabs. The last meal of a condemned beast. I reckon he thinks he's in heaven, only now he's going to get shot. I can't see any other outcome. Maybe I shouldn't have left him here, but it wasn't my fault the cage broke, was it?

A white van turns up and two blokes and a woman get out. They're all wearing green uniforms. They're carrying big, long bags. I reckon they're from a zoo or something because the police let them through the lines. They disappear into the factory. Now, that is brave.

I wish I could get closer. It feels wrong for me to be stuck up here, away from the action. He's my boy. I have this dream of me walking through the crowd and going in through that small gray door. Someone hands me a chicken. I find him, weak and bleeding and deadly, crouching under the mincing machine. I hold out the chicken and he trots after me like a dog. Everyone gasps. I lead him outside and through the parking lot and the crowd parts to let us pass. I throw the chicken in the cage and he follows. The door is locked. Carol has seen the whole thing and runs to kiss me. Josie joins her.

I want to be a hero.

I finger the tear in my coat.

Maybe I'll stay here.

* * *

211

It's nearly an hour later and people are getting bored. I scan the crowd but I can't see Josie. I don't know if she still works here. I hope not. Nothing new is happening. I can't hear him anymore. I hope they haven't killed him. At least they haven't brought out a body yet. His or anyone else's. Yes, it's getting quieter every minute. People aren't running around like they were before. I wonder if I should change my position. There might be a window farther around. Maybe I could get in. I have to know what is happening.

The crowd has fallen silent again.

I know what this is. It's white noise.

I want to put my fingers in my ears but I don't. I have to face this. I am shivering. I am freezing. Poor Beast. He hates the cold.

I'm sorry, boy.

There is the sound of a deadened shot.

EPILOGUE

I'm up here in our favorite place, watching the shoppers in High Street. I look at the cracked tiles on the roofs and the disused chimney pots. Do you remember how we pretended to be Supermen and jumped from building to building? I was never very good at that, was I? Remember that woman who looked up and saw us one time? I was expecting abuse, but she only smiled and walked on. We once had a long conversation up here about how we were going to get out of this country and run us a beach bar in the Bahamas. I might still do that. I'll call it Selby's. How about that? Hey, I'm the same age as you now. Mad.

You know, I'm glad I followed you out that night. The night you died. I knew you'd be in the parking lot with your mates, Arnie Perch and Matt Glissons. I also knew you'd tell me where to go if you saw me. You didn't like me hanging round when you were doing that stuff. But I was there, all right. I was behind the frozen-food truck. It's always there on a Friday night. I was sitting there watching you lot messing around. Maybe you knew I was there all along. I saw you do that stuff. I saw you drinking.

I was deciding whether it was worth a thump to come and ask for a can. I came out from behind the truck when you fell over. Your mates were all laughing. But I wasn't. I knew something was wrong.

"He's not breathing." That's what Arnie said. And he and Matt ran off.

Did you know I sat in all that mess and held your head? I told you stuff too, I told you about my boy. I thought when you came round you'd have forgotten. But you didn't come round. And when the paramedics came I was still there and they had to pull me away so they could do the resuscitation.

I only went to your grave twice, Selby. Once for the funeral and once a few years ago. But you weren't there. I couldn't feel you. Up here, on the roof. This is where you are.

My boy lived, can you believe it? I saw it on telly at the Reynoldses'. It was all there on the screen. They were all set to destroy him but someone noticed his movements were getting slower and that he was making less noise. The reptile expert from the zoo figured it out. The factory was too cold for my boy. He couldn't cope and he just shut down. He found himself a hidey-hole in the basement and went into a kind of coma and they were able to tranq him. I'm not surprised the cold nearly killed him. It nearly killed me when I was working there. The zoo has him, but only temporarily. They say they haven't got the facilities. On the telly it said that when he gets better he's going to be flown right out of this country back to India where he is going to be kept in a special enclosure. They say they can't release him into the wild because he doesn't know how to hunt as someone has been keeping him in captivity. That's a laugh, isn't it? Sure, he can hunt. We know that. He hunted me!

There's national speculation about where he's come from. Everyone's talking about it. Of course I haven't said anything, and neither have the others. Not yet anyway. People are saying all sorts of crazy things. One bloke reckoned my boy was part of a terrorist plot. Someone else said he may have escaped from an illegal crocodile-skin farm. And there was this wildlife expert on the telly who swore the crocodile had swum across the sea in a warm stream of water or something. He said it was a warning sign that the earth was getting hotter. Everyone has something to say about it. One of the newspapers started calling him the Kebab Croc, and the name has stuck.

I saw him on telly and I swear he looked right at me.

I can't believe no one has blamed me yet. I get done for everything else that goes wrong. And while we're on the subject, no it wasn't me who set fire to St. Mark's. It was an accident, caused by some piss head setting fire to his bed with his cigarette.

I've been allowed to stay on at the Reynoldses', but not for long. Jimmy has sorted it for me to go and work for his brother. This brother lives near Aberdeen and has a fishing boat. Jimmy says I should just go there for a couple of months for a change of scene.

It's like he knows.

Who I am trying to fool? The real reason Jimmy wants me out of the way is because I'm getting rather friendly with his daughter, if you know what I mean. I can't see it lasting. I know what she's really like. But I'm sure as hell enjoying it while I can. Last night, I slept right through. There were no dreams, good or bad. I can't remember when that last happened.

I went to say good-bye to Eric. I was nervous, but he's not mad at me anymore. He's started making weather vanes. He

215

showed me the one he was working on. There's a steel arrow that can spin north, south, east, or west. He'd made a spine that goes up and he said he was going to fix an animal to it. He scrabbled around his toolbox to find it. I expected him to bring out a chicken or something but instead he showed me a black metal crocodile.

He's given me the weather vane. One day I might have a house to fix it to. Or maybe I'll fix it to the beach bar in the Bahamas.

I'm not going to bother Gran or Chas by saying good-bye. And Mum won't know any different. And Dad, well, he's just off on another one of his walkabouts, isn't he? He'll turn up again. He always does. So it's only you I've got to say good-bye to. I thought this would be the best place to do it. I've got my car and one hundred pounds to get up to Scotland. But before I go, there's something I have to do.

The sun is shining through the leaves on to the grass. There are blue flowers everywhere. Birds are singing and it's warm enough for me to wear just a T-shirt and jeans. The ground is dry. It's amazing how the weather can change in just a few days. It seems like ages since I was here last, though it was only a month ago. In places where trees have been cut down, all the green stuff is growing up and I have to fight my way through. The air smells good and fresh, like a clean bathroom.

I reach the clearing with the hut. I brush dead leaves and twigs from the hammock. It hasn't been used for ages. A plank in the roof of the hut has come away and as I get near a couple of pigeons fly out. Inside, a furry mold coats half a cabbage and a carton of rancid milk sits on the floor.

I hear a noise and go outside. Passing around to the back of the hut I am biting my lip. It could be my imagination. I'm slightly mad now, you know. Ever since the meat factory parking lot, things feel different. Like the world has shifted to one side. Like my eyesight has changed. I can't explain it. But it makes life feel smoother.

I see him.

He's so thin he looks like a starvation victim. He's too weak to move far, but there's a stagnant bucket of water he must have been drinking from. Just enough to keep him alive. There's rubbish all around. Turds and food, a broken-open box of cookies, a wrapper of ham. A bread bag.

"Poor old bugger," I say gently, and touch his head. He looks up at me and sighs. His coat is wet through. I wonder how he hasn't died of exposure. I reckon he's been out here for nearly two weeks. I untie my top from around my waist and wrap it around him.

I loosen the rope. It's so tight it's bitten right into him. The skin is red and raw underneath. I only allow myself to think briefly of what it must have been like tied up out here, day after day, night after night, on his own, slowly starving to death.

"It's going to be all right," I say. "I'm back. I'm looking after you now."

I pick him up and hug him to my chest. He's so light.

"Come on, Malackie, my boy," I say. "Let's go."